THE NAME'S
BUCHANAN

G·K
Hall
&Cͦͅ

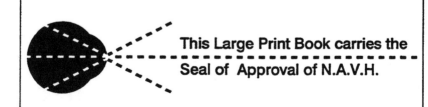

This Large Print Book carries the
Seal of Approval of N.A.V.H.

THE NAME'S BUCHANAN

JONAS WARD

G.K. Hall & Co.
Thorndike, Maine

Published in 1995 by arrangement with
Golden West Literary Agency.

All characters in this book are fictional and any resemblance to persons living or dead is purely coincidental.

G.K. Hall Large Print Western Collection.

The text of this Large Print edition is unabridged.
Other aspects of the book may vary from the original edition.

Set in 16 pt. News Plantin.

Printed in the United States on permanent paper.

Library of Congress Cataloging in Publication Data

Ward, Jonas, 1939–
    The name's Buchanan / Jonas Ward.
        p.   cm.
    ISBN 0-7838-1471-2 (lg. print : hc)
    1. Large type books.   I. Title.
[PS3557.A715N36   1995]
813'.54—dc20   95-24496

THE NAME'S
BUCHANAN

CHAPTER ONE

IT was Gomez who was first aware that something was wrong. Very wrong. He did not waste time or words to send someone else but rode off himself to intercept the riderless horse. A short and solid old man in full possession of his faculties, Gomez knew even at this distance what horse it was and whose horse it was. He had foaled the coal-black filly himself, supervised its special rearing, and been privileged by Don Pedro to present it in person to Maria on her sixteenth birthday, two years before. So he knew that horse very well; knew it, you might almost say, to speak to.

"What is this?" he growled in Spanish when he had scooped the black's loose reins into his fist and brought it up short. "Where do you go without the mistress?" Now he dismounted and circled the animal, looking first for a note of explanation that the young girl might have sent back, then for a message of any kind that she might have scratched onto the leather of the saddle. But there was none, and he could detect nothing in the filly's appearance to indicate what had happened. The animal's coat was not lathered from a hard run, nor was she wall-eyed. Even so, the realistic Gomez suspected the worst, and the worst in this part of California was that the horse had been startled by a rattler, thrown its rider and sped off. Then, with the danger behind and forgotten, it had simply wandered back to the ranch.

Gomez remounted his own big-chested stallion and drove both horses in the direction of the sprawling hacienda that was winter headquarters of Rancho del Rey. Gomez and his men worked her the year 'round, but Don Pedro moved his family to the seaside near Agua Caliente during the hot season. In fact, Gomez reflected absently now, it was in Caliente that Maria was going to be married this coming June. *Madre Mia,* where have the years flown to?

By this time all work had stopped on the place, and the sight of the black without its familiar, vivacious rider was so disquieting that no one dared put his private fears into words. The household had been alerted, so that Don Pedro and Doña Isabel hurried out onto the terrace to meet their segundo.

"What has happened to my daughter?" the owner asked with the stiff formality that was his chief trait.

"Truly, señor," Gomez answered, "I do not yet know. I would request permission to start a search."

"Granted," Don Pedro said, his voice betraying no emotion. But as his wife Isabel knew, and as his friend Gomez knew, the more turmoil that stirred in the old don's breast the colder was the front that he presented to the world. A tall and slender man, an aristocrat in the old world and a true *cabellero* in the new, Pedro Francisco del Cuervo lived by a code of manners and morals that made its strictest demands on himself.

With a bow to Doña Isabel, Gomez wheeled his mount and proceeded toward the fenced corral at a trot, issuing orders as soon as the waiting men were within earshot. But his own segundo, Ramon, had anticipated him and an even dozen top vaqueros were already in the saddle awaiting directions. Gomez led them in a body down the great, curving cobblestone roadway that connected the hacienda with the many wagon trails that reached out to all parts of the ranch like spokes of a wheel. At the point in the road which formed the hub of this wheel, Gomez halted the party and then sent them off in pairs along each of the six trails, any one of which a carefree and beautiful young girl might have chosen for her daily ride.

Gomez himself, with a great anxiety in his heart, rode the public trail that led to Agrytown, just across the border in the state of California.

Buchanan had passed that way just half an hour before, heading in the same direction — away from Mexico. After two years, Tom Buchanan and Mexico had had enough of one another. Buchanan wanted to get away from the great hellhole that was the state of Sonora, and in particular from that lying, cheating Campos who called himself General of the People's Army and *El Libertad.* All that Campos wanted to liberate was the government treasury, and Buchanan wondered again why it had taken him two long, weary years to find out what a phony revolution he had got mixed up in.

No, he and Campos wouldn't miss each other. Nor would the government, whose troops he had harassed and raided all those dirty months. Oh, maybe there was a *chiquita* here and a *chiquita* there who might still be able to stand the sight of him — and vice-versa, especially in San Javier. How could such a God-forsaken little town produce so many amiable women?

Something just as incongruous as the girls of San Javier attracted Buchanan's attention then, and as saddle-weary as he was after twelve hours' steady riding, he became instantly alert. A horse was flying down the road toward him, going to beat hell. But it carried no rider to rake its side with spurs or quirt it.

Buchanan put his own tired animal squarely across the trail, pulled his battered hat from his head and flagged the oncoming black first to a trot and then to a halt. As Gomez was to do a little later, Buchanan inspected the filly carefully, also looking for a message of some kind, but inspecting horseflesh as well. This was somebody's fine property, he thought, and for a moment the temptation was in him. Then, with a hard slap at the filly's rump, he sent her on her way again and wondered how much influence *El Libertad* had had on him to make him even consider horse stealing.

It's you for the States, Buchanan, he told himself fiercely, and never leave them again. Even so, the incident of meeting the horse troubled him and his eyes searched this way and that as he resumed his traveling. There was a fork up ahead and Buchanan took the more northerly of the roads.

It was a mile beyond the fork that his glance caught a gleam of something white off the trail. He halted and dismounted, leaving the horse while he made his way on foot through the heavy brush. The stuff was thick, but it appeared as though someone had recently come through here from the opposite direction, biding it all toward him. Then he reached the thing he had seen, a piece of torn white lace — good Spanish lace if Buchanan was any judge — caught on a bramble. He left it there and pushed further on. Abruptly the sharp and thorny foliage ended and he was on the bank of a stream. Directly in front of him a girl was lying face down in the water, her black hair spread out like a great fan, and the whole of her body looking ill-used and lifeless.

Buchanan lifted her onto the bank, saw that at least she had not yet swallowed her tongue and located a faint beat beneath her breast. He went to work at what he knew fundamentally was the way to force the water out of her lungs. For fifteen minutes he labored over her, pushing and squeezing beneath her exposed ribs, and almost a cupful of water came out of her before his ears were rewarded with a moaning sound

11

from deep in her chest. In another five minutes she was breathing in almost regular fashion, but she did not regain consciousness and Buchanan knew that was because of the bloody gash someone had opened at the base of her skull.

What else had been done to her here could only be guessed at from the evidence of her torn clothing, as well as the signs of struggle in the uprooted grass and the very piece of lace that had led him here. That, he guessed, had been carried away unknowingly by her attacker and then been caught in passing by the bramble.

If he wasn't sure that Luis Campos was four hundred miles to the south of here — Buchanan broke off the thought, telling himself bitterly that there were other scum in this world besides Campos.

Now the problem was to get her warm. He went away and returned with his own blanket, an item as faded and threadbare as the clothes on his back, wrapped her in it snugly and lifted her in his arms. Such a wisp of a thing, Buchanan thought. And a good strong face. He would have to call her something more than just pretty . . . Buchanan looked up to find himself staring down the unwavering barrel of a handgun. The gun was an American Colt, like the pair hanging at his own hips, but the toter was a Mexican — a capable-looking old man with gray-black *mostachos* and the appearance of great strength in his face.

"Hombre," Gomez said in Spanish, "what are

you doing with that girl?"

Buchanan considered his answer carefully, marking well the deep emotion in the old man's voice.

"Padre," he said in Spanish, "this one has had trouble. But I am a stranger to it."

Gomez believed him, just like that. But he believed him because he had spoken just as he had, with the same sorrow, for to come upon the Señorita Maria in the arms of such a formidable character as this was to suspect the worst. He was tall, taller by a head than Don Pedro, with the look of a wild animal in his battered, unshaven face. An ominous type to meet on the trail, Gomez thought. Even now he is still recovering from what must have been an almost fatal beating.

Gomez reholstered the gun, nevertheless. "I will part the bushes for you, señor," he said and led the way back.

Buchanan followed, grateful for the help and noting that the man now addressed him as señor instead of hombre. "Is this girl your daughter?" he asked.

"She is like my daughter," Gomez answered. "She is Maria del Cuervo. I am segundo to her father."

"Some man has been very cruel with her," Buchanan said.

Gomez turned to look up into Buchanan's face. They gazed at each other for a long moment and then Gomez resumed the journey to where their horses waited. Buchanan thought, This is the kind

13

of man I've been making life miserable for these past two years — a nice, decent guy wanting nothing but peace. "Can you ride with her?"

Buchanan nodded. "If you will hold her while I mount." Gomez took the blanketed form in his arms, returned it when Buchanan was in his saddle. Then Gomez lifted the reins over the horse's head, mounted his own and led the slow procession back toward the hacienda. They were met, however, just beyond the fork in the road, by a party of horsemen and one who drove a team and wagon.

"You have found her!" shouted a young man among them, one who was dressed better and who sat his horse straighter than the others. He was Juan del Cuervo, Maria's brother, and he rode directly to Buchanan.

"How is she? Is she all right?"

"She's alive," Buchanan said.

"The horse threw her? She struck her head?"

Buchanan glanced at Gomez, who shook his head, Buchanan shrugged his shoulders in answer to the question. He handed the girl down to two men who carried her very tenderly to the wagon. Juan del Cuervo handed his reins to someone else and climbed in beside his sister. The trip was resumed.

It was when they were on the cobblestone entranceway that Gomez thought to ask the stranger his name and an account of his finding the señorita so that all could be related properly to Don Pedro and Doña Isabel. But, unaccountably, Buchanan was no longer with them.

That was strange behavior, Gomez thought and then he gave the matter more consideration. Perhaps it was just as well, the old man told himself. The stranger was most probably *un hombre muy malo,* and Don Pedro being the *caballero* that he was, he would most certainly feel a lifetime debt. It was not natural that gentlemen should be obliged to rogues, Gomez decided. Nor should a gentleman's highborn daughter be discomforted by a wayfarer's intimate knowledge of her misfortune. It was better for everyone that the man was gone from their lives as quickly as he had entered them.

CHAPTER TWO

TIA ROSA, the midwife, made the first examination of the unconscious girl, cut the matted hair from the deep scalp wound, bandaged it and held her own counsel until Dr. Alvarez arrived from the town. When the doctor was finished he agreed with the midwife's findings and Don Pedro was summoned.

"Please, my friend, seat yourself," the doctor said.

"I will stand, Alfredo. Is my daughter gravely injured?

"Physically," Dr. Alvarez began slowly, "Maria will have a full recovery. She has the strength of her father."

"We are only what God makes us."

"Very true. But there is another thing, another injury suffered by your daughter. It is something that may have damaged her spirit, something that will make her require your guidance and understanding as never before. . . ."

"What are you trying to tell me?"

"The girl has been violated, Don Pedro," Alvarez told him gently, and there was a long and stunning silence.

"My daughter?" the proud father said icily. "Such a thing is unthinkable."

"But, unfortunately, a fact."

"You have, of course, informed no one else of this?"

"Only yourself."

"And you two — I have your pledge of secrecy?"

The doctor and the frightened midwife nodded.

"Time," Alvarez said, "heals all wounds. What I prescribe for Maria is gentleness and understanding."

Don Pedro silenced him with a gesture. "Thank you, Alfredo," he said. "You will call on your patient regularly?"

"I will be here the first thing tomorrow morning." The doctor left the hacienda then and returned to town. Don Pedro went to his study, and after an hour had passed he called his wife and son into the room.

"Our name has been dishonored," he told them. "Against her will, a man has had carnal knowledge of our beloved Maria."

A sob broke spontaneously from Doña Isabel. Juan del Cuervo went white beneath his tanned complexion.

"I will kill him very slowly," Juan said.

"You will kill whom, my son?"

"I will find him out, never fear."

"And you will then announce your reasons for killing him?"

"I —" The young man's voice broke off abruptly. He shook his head. "My sister must be avenged."

17

"In good time, Juan," his father said. "In good time."

"Immediately! He cannot live a minute longer than I can manage his death."

"No," Doña Isabel said, brushing away her tears. "This is a very delicate matter. Your sister intends to be married in a few short months." She looked at her husband. "I, personally, have never given my full approval to young Sebastian, nor to the Diaz family. But Maria is apparently fond of him, and the alliance is advantageous —"

"Sebastian Diaz is Maria's choice," Don Pedro said angrily. "I am not bargaining with my daughter's happiness."

"Of course not, dear husband." The woman turned to her son. "But you know Sebastian very well, Juan. We have all seen him grow from a rather willful little boy to one of the wealthiest young men in all of Mexico —"

"But what has this to do with Maria's betrayer?" the young man interrupted impetuously.

"A great deal," Isabel said, "if your sister truly loves Sebastian. Sebastian is used to having everything come to him new, firsthand." She glanced down into her lap and the rosary interlaced in her fingers. "Wrong or right," she said, "Sebastian would demand that he bring a maiden to the wedding bed."

"But Maria is!"

"In her heart, yes. In God's knowledge. But should Sebastian learn of this terrible incident of today — I am not so certain of his sympathy,

18

of his understanding."

"To hell with Sebastian!" Juan shouted. "Let Maria find a man of heart —"

"You are young," Don Pedro told him sternly. "Your blood runs hot in your veins and needs cooling."

"Your father speaks truly," Doña Isabel said gently. "You are twenty years old, you are not thinking of marriage. When you do, you will see how your thinking has been disciplined to the customs of our time."

"I would never hold — rape — against my bride's honor."

"Then you would be one man in a thousand in Mexico," his mother said.

Juan sat down then, and seemed to subside.

Don Pedro said, "We will, in time, learn the man's identity. Then, with Maria married, and without her knowledge, we will do what must be done."

Juan raised his head, was about to speak out, then closed his lips in a tight line.

"Maria," Don Pedro continued, "is still not conscious. Tia Rosa will attend her, and Juan, I desire that you and Gomez stand alternate watch outside the door. The girl may suffer delirium and no one must hear her outcries under any circumstances. Do you understand, my son?"

Juan nodded, got up and left his parents alone to discuss the thing further. He climbed to the floor above and took up his station outside the door of his sister's room. Three hours later Gomez arrived to spell him.

"Café," the young man said affectionately, calling the segundo by the nickname he had earned from his constant drinking of coffee, "Café, where is the man who carried Maria in his arms when we met you this afternoon?"

"He went on his way, Señor Juan."

"His way where? Why?"

"Who knows?"

"I remember him," Juan said. "I paid little attention at the time, but now I think of him. He was a hard-looking man. He said practically nothing."

"*Un vago*. A type that moves from place to place, and never tarries."

"Which way was he moving today?"

"Toward the border." Gomez looked intently at Juan. "But you are wrong if you suspect him of this thing."

"Then you know?"

"I know what I know. The hombre also knew, but he was not the one."

"You are very certain."

"As certain as I am that it was not myself."

Juan left Gomez then, to eat his supper and, presumably, to sleep. For this was the time of the winter roundup, and this season Don Pedro had elevated Juan to range boss — under Gomez' supervision, of course, but boss just the same and coming gradually into his own as *primo* of the Rancho del Rey. It was early to bed and early to rise at roundup season, but the young boss did not bed down, although he returned to his rooms in the west wing. While there he looked over his collection of handguns and rifles, finally chose a Remington .45 and a carbine, and whiled away an hour cleaning both weapons, testing their action and then loading them with live ammunition. He opened a bottle of Franciscan brandy then, lit a cigar borrowed from his father's private stock, and in the presence of guns, liquor and tobacco saw himself as a man full-grown and specially dedicated.

He thought of Maria, and so many memories of his younger sister flooded his mind that he had to herd them into a sensible whole, a complete picture. He passed over the annoyances of their early youth, the demands that a little sister can make on the activities and the patience of a boy two years older. He forgot how she demanded, and got, equality in all things, how she made him wonder who was the elder and who the younger, who the son in this patriarchal system and who the daughter with no other problem but to get safely married.

Tonight Juan didn't think of the strong-minded Maria but of the smiling, agreeable, sweet-scented and always feminine little sister that one could not consider without a happy little pang tugging at the heart. She was so good, so beautiful — so innocent — that it reduced one to sentimental extremes to see her.

And some man had debased her. Some terrible person, male like himself, had attacked Maria and brought dishonor to the name of Del Cuervo.

Juan finished the brandy in his glass and moved down the great corridor of the hacienda toward the room where Maria lay. Gomez straightened at his approach.

"*Que va?*"

"I just wanted to see her for a few moments," Juan explained, opening the door swiftly. He went inside and closed the door behind him. Tia Rosa sat in a padded rocking chair near the bed, but the chair was motionless and when Juan investigated he found the old woman drowsing. Good. He leaned down over his sister's pale face.

"Maria," he whispered. "Maria!"

There was an answering sound from the girl's lips.

"Maria — can you hear me?"

"Yes," came the toneless answer.

"Who did this to you, Maria? Who was he?"

"Ro—" the voice started to say, then stopped.

"Roy?" Juan asked insistently. "Roy Agry?"

"Yes." Suddenly the girl's eyelids fluttered open. She looked around wonderingly. "What happened? Where —"

But her brother was already across the room, opening the door. The sounds awoke Tia Rosa who gave a startled cry; the woman arose and went to the bedside.

Gomez, too, was disturbed. Not by anything he had heard but by the look on the face of Don Pedro's son.

"What is it, Juan? What has happened?"

The young man walked away without speaking, returned to his rooms for the guns, and left the great house by a rear door. He cut out his own sleek stallion from the remuda, saddled it and rode down the cobblestone drive. From there he took the public road that led to Agrytown across the border.

CHAPTER THREE

AGRYTOWN looked as good as any place to Buchanan for a meal and a bed. He admitted that the town had a flimsy look to it, an impermanence, but then he realized that just five short years ago all this had been part of Mexico, too. Give us Americans a chance, he told himself. We're starting from scratch.

The big man grinned a little wryly at his use of the word "we." For every place he looked in Agrytown seemed to be claimed by Agry, whoever he was. The Agry Hotel, Agry's Mercantile, Agry's Saloon, Agry's Livery — why he'd even read a notice pertaining to the use of firearms signed by "Lew Agry, High Sheriff." And now, as he entered the lobby of the small hotel he was greeted by an electioneering poster: "Vote for Simon Agry for U. S. Senator." Agrytown was a closed corporation for sure.

"I need a room for the night," Buchanan told the clerk.

"Ten dollars, in advance."

"That all?"

"Take it or leave it."

What Buchanan wanted to take was one short, swift swing at the fat face before him. But hell, he was too happy to be back in the States for any ramstamming like that. He opened the ragged shortcoat to reveal a splendid leather belt fastened by a huge, solid silver buckle. Tied above the belt was a leather purse, and Buchanan dipped his fingers inside and brought forth a gold coin worth fifty dollars.

"Wrong one," he said and put it back. On the fourth try he located a ten-dollar gold piece which he flipped negligently to the desk. The wide-eyed clerk picked up the coin and dropped it on the steel bar beside the register. The gold gave a fine, solid ring and then it disappeared into the safe. Buchanan signed the book.

"First room at the head of the stairs, mister," the clerk said, his glance shifting from Buchanan's unshaven, abused face to the surprising leather purse.

"I'll use it later. Where's some good grub in town?"

"They'll cook you up a steak over to the saloon. Tell 'em Amos sent you."

"You an Agry?" Buchanan asked innocently.

"I'm a cousin. Why'd you ask?"

"Curious by nature," Buchanan said and went out and across the dirt street to the Agry Saloon. There was a noisy ruckus in progress at the bar between a young, big-shouldered man and the bartender, to which everyone was paying what Buchanan thought was unusually close attention.

"You pa give me strict orders about your drinking, Roy," the bartender was saying nervously.

"Put another bottle up, by hell," the one named Roy said, "or I'll come back there and take it."

"You don't want me to lose my job, do you?"

"Who in hell cares about you? I'm Roy Agry and I want a bottle!"

"I can't do it, Roy."

"How about me?" Buchanan asked, shouldering his way in. "Can I get a steak?"

"Who do you think you're shovin' there, jaspar?" Roy Agry said, but when he angrily tried to move Buchanan aside nothing happened. He grabbed the arm of the ragged coat and jerked at it. The arm came back, fast, and the point of Buchanan's elbow jammed itself into the pit of Agry's belly, knocking him off balance. Agry gave a sharp grunt.

"That steak ought to be cooked so the meat's still on the red side," Buchanan continued to the bartender. "But don't you give me no meal that's out-and-out raw . . ."

The bartender wasn't even listening. He was looking at something that was happening beyond Buchanan's shoulder. Roy Agry had a long-barreled .44 in his hand, upraised to bring it down on Buchanan's head. Buchanan saw the situation in the back-bar mirror and moved with cat-like grace to avoid the skulling. The descending gun grazed his ear and slammed down onto the bar. Buchanan hit Agry twice for that, once in the belly, once on the point of his lantern jaw. Agry's legs quit supporting him and he went down in a clumsy heap.

"Man, you're full of vinegar tonight," Buchanan told him conversationally, hoisting Agry back to his feet. As he did he noticed the long scratches on the other man's cheeks, four on each side, stretching from his eye to his neck. Those marks made Buchanan think of something else that had happened, but for the moment he couldn't place the memory. His embarrassment was too great, anyhow, to let him dwell on the matter, and as he propped Roy Agry against the bar he scolded himself mentally for brawling with a fellow American on his first night back in the States.

"I'll kill you, you son of a bitch," Roy Agry said in a blurred voice. Buchanan grinned at him.

"First let me buy you a drink," he said.

"No more drinks for him," the bartender announced. "And if I was you, friend, I'd light out of this town quick."

"Too late," Buchanan said. "I already bought my room. Now how about that bottle and how about that nice steak?"

The barman shrugged. "I'm selling this to you, mister," he said loud enough for all to hear, setting a quart of The Lion's Roar rye whisky in front of Buchanan. "That'll be ten dollars."

"Man," Buchanan said, parting the shortcoat again, "I'm sure glad I'm not settling down in this ten-dollar town permanent." He fished down into the purse, and after several mistries finally located a twenty-dollar coin. "How much for the steak?" he asked.

"Ten dollars."

Buchanan tossed him the gold money, reminding himself forcibly how grateful he was to be back. Then he offered the bottle to Roy Agry.

"After you, old horse," he said.

Agry grabbed the liquor from Buchanan's hand, tilted it to his lips and drank thirstily. Almost desperately, Buchanan thought. "Save a drop," he said. "I've built up a small hankerin' myself."

The bartender had hollered out back somewhere for the steak and now he swung to Buchanan. "Why don't you take the bottle to a table by yourself?" he asked nervously. "You're just piling up charges for yourself with the whole Agry family."

"Not my intention," Buchanan said, "but I'll do whatever you want me to." He looked at Agry for the return of the bottle.

"You've got till this is empty," Roy said, holding it to his chest. "After that, you lousy bum, I'm gonna kill you."

Buchanan frowned, and his shoulders shifted impatiently.

"Your steak's coming off the fire in a minute," the bartender said in his anxious voice. "Eat it and get out of here."

Buchanan made himself smile. "Whatever you say," he told the barman good-naturedly, and moved away to a table in the far corner. The other customers looked at him curiously, kept watching all the while he ate and drank his coffee. It was as if they were present at a very unusual wake.

Buchanan was oblivious to it all, so disappointed was he in the quality of the food. Perhaps, he thought, he'd looked forward to his first meal in the States with too much expectation. Maybe he was too used to those damn spices and hot sauces back in Sonora. How that fat slob Campos used to fuss with his women about food!

He looked up to see how Roy Agry was coming with the bottle. Half gone, he saw. But by the time he was finished the man would be all gone himself. Who the hell wanted a gunfight, anyhow? Not him. Not Tommy Buchanan. Strictly a peaceful, peace loving citizen of the good old U.S.A. from now on. Which reminded him, for no good reason, that he was going to shave one of these days, soon as the face wasn't so bloody tender from what Campos and the boys had done to it.

Forget that, too, he said to himself. They beat up on you, but you gave as good as you got, especially to Campos. And you've still got your hard-earned money. Buchanan laughed aloud. By hell, Campos couldn't steal it but these unarmed thieves in Agrytown will. He stood up and walked back to the bar.

"My name is Buchanan," he said, ostensibly to the bartender, "and if anybody needs me I'm across the way at the hotel. First room at the top of the stairs, and the door will be off the latch." He went out then, crossed over to the hotel and mounted to his room. But instead of the bed he bunked down on the floor opposite, and he went off to sleep with the Colt in his fist and primed. . . .

29

By that time Roy Agry had forgotten about him. The other thing was too much in his mind, a nightmare that wouldn't let him escape, and it seemed that the more he drank to forget what he had done the more vivid his memories became.

It was as though he had known all along that he would come to do such a brutal and violent thing; as if one of those roving Mexican women had looked into the palm of his hand when he was a kid and said "Roy Agry, when you are twenty-one you are going to do a terrible thing to someone. . . ."

There was flash temper and violence in all the Agrys. His Uncle Lew, the sheriff, was no man to be around when he was mad. He remembered Uncle Lew horsewhipping Aunt Anna years ago. He remembered last week, when Uncle Lew shot and killed the half-breed for not getting out of his way on the duckboards. His father Simon, who owned the town and was going to be senator, had a different kind of violence in him. His temper was just as short as Lew's, he was just as quick to take offense, but he was slyer about it. He got even with people he didn't like in a quieter way. He let other people do his work and didn't leave himself open to criticism like his brother did.

Roy suspected he had a little of each of them in him. He had warned Maria when he'd heard of the coming marriage that no other man was going to have her. She thought he was bluffing, but he'd shown her. Just as Uncle Lew had shown

30

that breed. But like his father, he'd covered himself. There was only one witness — Maria — and he'd fixed it so she'd never talk against him.

Not that anything could be done to him. It had happened over in Mexico, hadn't it? This was Agrytown, state of California. Who could touch an Agry in his own town for what had been done to a Mex? Sure, that's all Maria was. A Mex. Still, it wasn't the kind of thing you want people talking about. Men acted funny about another man who'd —

He lifted the bottle and drank deeply from it. There it was again. What he'd said when he'd dragged her off the horse. What she'd said. Her fighting him, scratching him, screaming at him. His knocking her to the ground, hitting her with the gun. What he'd done then . . . From a great distance he heard someone calling his name.

"Roy Agry!" Juan shouted again from the saloon entrance. "Are you going to draw or be shot down like a dog?"

It was Maria's brother, Roy thought foggily. Maria's brother!

"There'll be none of that!" the bartender yelled, leveling a shotgun at Juan del Cuervo. "Get out of here, Mex!"

Juan could not know whether the bartender would fire the scattergun or not. He felt only the sting of the name Mex. It made him an outcast here, an interloper in the camp of his enemy's friends. So when he drew the Remington from its holster he fully expected to be killed in the

31

act. The big .45 came clear and jumped and roared death in Juan's slim hands until there was no more vengeance in it. Even then the smooth-working hammer clicked three times on empty shell cases.

It was all over in so many blurred seconds, but for Roy Agry those seconds had seemed an eternity. He had stared in fascination as Maria's brother had brought the gun into sight. He had still had a gunfighter's chance, but Roy was no gunfighter. He was the bullying, arrogant son of a rich and ruthless father. And he died in his father's saloon as he had lived in his father's long shadow: a coward.

The bartender never fired the rifle. In fact, when the Mexican youth's intentions were clear he had abandoned the gun and dived for safety behind his oaken barricade. Everyone else in the half-filled place had sought to get out of the way, too, with the result that Juan seemed to be the only man on his feet when the thing was done. Beyond this he had not planned at all, and now he was overwhelmed. He flung the gun away from him, turned and fled — straight into the arms of Waldo Peek, first deputy sheriff of Agry County. Peek had been in the cribhouse next door, trying out the Apache Indian girl, and he was bound for the saloon to tell the boys what a wildcat she was and how he'd tamed her. He'd heard the gunfire, but put it down to just one more liquored-up cowpoke shooting harmlessly at the bullet-studded ceiling. Instead, it was trouble —

that was Roy Agry pouring out his life's blood on the floor, and this Mex kid turning toward him was the killer. Waldo wrapped his bearlike arms around Juan's slim body and drove his thick knee into Juan's groin. The youth collapsed against him and Waldo gave it to him again. Then he held him at arm's length and beat his fist repeatedly into Juan's face. And the more he hit the boy the wilder his anger became, without reason, for among all those that Waldo hated in this world Roy Agry topped the list.

Buchanan came awake as if warned by some sixth sense — awake and scrambling to his feet even before Juan had finished emptying his gun into Roy Agry across the street. He went to the open window and looked out with a face that was frankly and actively curious.

Buchanan had been absorbed with everything that his fellow humans did since his childhood days in West Texas. People and events fascinated him, and there was nothing better than a gunfight unless it was a prairie fire. But what was going on over there wasn't fun at all to watch. The beefy hombre was much too much for the slender kid and before he realized what he was doing, Buchanan was dropping from the window to the tin overhang, then coming down from that to the street below.

He crossed the street in four long strides, wrenched Peek loose from his prisoner, and when the deputy swung on him Buchanan blocked the

33

blow with his raised elbow. Almost a part of the same defensive movement was the hard, overhand right that punched Peek's face out of proportion and scrambled his thinking. For good measure, and because he felt justified, Buchanan let go with the left hand. Waldo caught that one in the mouth, but even as he was being removed from the battle Buchanan was catching hell from behind.

All kinds of hell from a man who knew his business.

CHAPTER FOUR

THE pair of queens," Simon Agry said, "bets ten dollars." He slid the stack of ten chips into the sizable pot in the center of the poker table and leaned back into his chair with a wheezing sound. Gross was the word for the self-appointed mayor, judge and treasurer of Agrytown. Not big, gross. Simon stood six feet and six inches, without boots, and he needed every bit of it to move his three hundred pounds from one comfortable spot to another. His face was a great round thing, with dark, deep-sunken eyes, a fierce black beard and a head that was completely bald and gleaming now in the flickering gaslight of the chandelier. He was a lot of man, was Simon Agry, and everyone who knew him even passing well hated his ample guts. Including, and especially, his younger brother Lew, who sat across the table from him and was studying the pair of queens showing in Simon's stud hand and wondering what he had in the hole.

That was the damned trouble with Si, you never knew what he had in the hole. One hand he'd play conservative, the next wide open. He kept you off balance all the time. You never knew where you stood.

"I'll stay," Cousin Amos announced and Lew shifted his attention to that hand. All red cards,

35

a possible flush. Then the horse buyer from Chicago, Horace Willow, pushed his ten chips into the pile. Willow had been losing as heavily and steadily as Lew himself, and the pair of tens he showed didn't look like much to the sheriff.

"Ten," Lew Agry said, "and ten more." He had a king on the board and a king in the hole. What encouraged him to raise was that there wasn't another king in sight.

"Too steep for me," announced the man on his left. This was Abe Carbo, the gunman and gambler, and twenty dollars wasn't too steep for him at all. Carbo was Simon Agry's man, his Jack-of-all-trades, and in addition to keeping Simon unmolested by various disgruntled citizens he also kept an eye on Brother Lew, a sort of living, breathing reminder not to get too big for his britches.

Now Horace Willow dealt the cards all around, face up once more, and both Agrys got what they wanted — another queen for Simon, another king for Lew. Hapless Cousin Amos pulled a black trey and threw in his hand. The man from Chicago dealt himself the jack of hearts.

"The three queens," Simon Agry said, "bet ten dollars."

Willow shook his head, turned his cards over.

"Your ten," Lew Agry said, "and my ten."

Simon looked at his brother's kings almost angrily. "Raise it again," he said, shoving thirty dollars' worth of chips forward, sitting back and wheezing.

The sheriff met the raise and Willow dealt the last card, face down. Simon's enormous hand covered his card and slid it back over the one in the hole. He very deliberately read them. Lew let his new card lie and gave all his attention to his brother.

"Got the three kings, Lew?" Simon asked harshly.

"That's for you to find out, Si. What do you bet?"

"I check to you."

A rare smile touched Lew Agry's face. He glanced down at his remaining chips and pushed the pile of them into the pot.

"Ten times ten, Si. I bet a hundred dollars."

Simon Agry clamped down tight on the cigar in the corner of his mouth. "I call," he said, and when Lew's hand snaked toward his hole card, added: "And bump it another hundred."

The sheriff of Agry County was stunned. Immobilized. Simon had checked to him. That could only mean that his brother had the three queens and nothing else. But it hadn't. The greedy, grinning bastard had trapped him into betting his roll.

"I call," Lew Agry said.

"With what, Lew?" Simon asked juicily.

"So I'm light a hundred. Don't you trust me for it?"

"Sure I trust you, Lew. But what do you say you call my raise with that new stud out to your spread?"

"What new stud?" the sheriff said, shifting his eyes quickly to Abe Carbo, then back again to his brother. "What are you talking about?"

"The stallion you picked up across the border last week," Simon told him. "A fine piece of horseflesh, I'm told."

"And worth a lot more than one hundred dollars," Lew said, the veins in his temples throbbing spasmodically.

"Then you don't call my raise? I take the pot?"

The sheriff turned to Willow. "You're buying horses. I've got a thoroughbred Spanish stallion. How much?"

Simon Agry lifted his hand. "I don't think Mr. Willow wants to bid against me," he said. "That horse is worth one hundred dollars. Fish, Lew, or cut bait."

"I bet the horse," Lew said in a tight, cold voice.

Simon smiled. "Four queens," he said, overturning the hole-card lady. "What have you got, Lew?"

"My bellyful," was the sullen answer.

"Abe'll come by for the stud tomorrow —" The gunfire broke across his voice and he instantly gripped the table in fear. Instinctively his brother and Abe Carbo came to their feet, hands sweeping back to loose-holstered guns. Lew Agry was a mockery of the star on his chest, but there was no fear in him. With Carbo it was different. He was paid to take his chances.

"Now what?" Lew said, going to the curtained

window of the hotel's card room and peering out into the night.

"It's someone after that hardcase," Cousin Amos said excitedly. "He went and showed that purse full of gold pieces!"

Lew saw his deputy approaching the saloon. He saw the Mexican kid run out and get himself manhandled. Lew grinned. That Waldo knew how to handle 'em. A form dropped down into view as if from the sky. A big man, running, and there was no mistaking his intent. Then the sheriff moved, moved out of the room and out of the hotel. And as he crossed the street the rage just boiled over in him. It wasn't only that justice was being interfered with, it was also his anger at his brother, at losing the money and the blood horse.

He hooked his arm around Buchanan's windpipe, put the point of his knee into Buchanan's spine, pulled back with the one while he shoved forward with the other. This was the way he had learned to fight from the Apache. This he had learned the hard way, campaigning with Zach Taylor's army against that devil Sant' Anna three years ago.

Buchanan knew it, too, and he knew that the harder he fought to break out of the grip the better his chances were to have his spinal column snapped in two. The thing to do was give with the pressure, but God, how do you *give* when the very air is being cut off from your windpipe? Add to that the slowly rising figure of Waldo

Peek, a hard, ugly man with murder in his little pig-eyes. Waldo's fist smashed into the bridge of a nose already broken a week ago by *El Libertad's* gun butt. Waldo's other fist wiped out what repairs time had made to Buchanan's splintered rib. Waldo kept at it until his arms were too weary and his knuckles bled. Then Lew Agry let go and Buchanan toppled head first into the dirt before the saloon.

CHAPTER FIVE

THE L-shaped adobe building had once been the guardhouse for a Mexican Army outpost stationed here, and though a section of the flat roof had been demolished by a cannon during the recent war, the place still served as the ten-cell Agrytown jail. On the rough stone floor of one of the cells, over which the roof was firmly intact, the disillusioned ex-revolutionist and soldier of misfortune named Thomas MacGrail Buchanan came painfully back to his senses. The whole experience had a familiarity about it, as though Buchanan were reliving his life, and when he felt of his midsection it was just as it had been on several occasions during the past two years. The belt with its magnificent silver buckle was gone. The purse with its little gold fortune was gone. His body and face were just one long bruise and he was right back where he had started.

Something passed across his chest and scurried away.

"Hell!" Buchanan said fervently. "Even the same lousy rats!" Ache as it did to move his head, the big man made himself rise first to a kneeling position and then a full stand. Buchanan was not a delicate type, but he did prefer to be on his feet in the company of rats.

"Quien es aquí?" asked a quavering, sick-sound-

ing young voice from the utter darkness.

"Who's yourself?" growled Buchanan uncompanionably in English. "And keep your bloody distance." This from previous experience in unlighted jails with many strange derelicts of humanity.

"I think you are the one who helped me tonight," Juan del Cuervo said haltingly in Buchanan's native tongue. Then, reverting emotionally to Spanish, "I am much obliged, friend."

"Sure. Are you on a bed, or something?"

"No. On the ground — on the floor."

"You better get up. Goddam rats'll go for your throat."

"I'll try again," Juan said, and as he struggled to rise Buchanan began to make out the slim figure on the opposite side of the little cell. He made his way there, reached down and got a hand under the younger man's armpit.

"Please, no," Juan said. "*Por favor*. I would do this thing myself."

"Sure," Buchanan said, thinking about these Mexicans and their posturing. Even Campos, the night he was gut-shot at Nuri, had snarled when Buchanan tried to help him remount. Proud, ugly bastard had to do it himself. But now, as he listened to this kid's muffled groans, watched him get to one knee, Buchanan had an embarrassing revelation about himself. Not if he knew it would any man ever have to raise him to his feet. Now what the hell put a crazy thought like that in his head?

"I made it," Juan said. "I think."

"Good for you," Buchanan said, made briefly surly by his feeling of guilt. He moved away then toward the third wall, out of memory, and felt for the bunk that should be there. It was.

"Come on over here," he said. "At least there's something to sit on." He lowered himself gratefully onto the iron cot with its loose straw mattress and made room for Juan.

"Got any tobacco?"

"I don't use it, señor." There was great sorrow in Juan's voice and Buchanan shifted uncomfortably.

"How come you're in the calaboose?" he asked. "It was you getting the licking."

"I killed a man tonight," Juan said simply. "I am here for that."

There it was again, Buchanan thought, with irritation. The dignity.

"With a knife?" he asked, his voice accusing.

"With a gun," Juan said. "Very badly."

"What do you mean, badly?"

"There was an interruption. I did not let Agry draw —"

"What Agry?"

"Roy, the son of Señor Simon."

"Why, hell, he was drunk."

The kid sighed. "I did not know," he said unhappily. "Even so, it would have made no difference."

"You must be a tiger for sure," Buchanan said. "What's your handle, anyhow?"

43

"Juan. Juan del Cuervo. What is your name?"

"Buchanan," Buchanan said negligently. It was not so common a name, Del Cuervo, that you could hear it twice in one day and fail to make the connection. He even remembered this Juan now, the excited one who rode like a young don and took over the arrangements for getting the girl home. He had left the party soon after Juan joined it, taken advantage of a sharp curve in the trail to swing around and get back on the road that led out of Mexico.

"How's the little girl?" he asked.

Juan's head came up sharply. Now he was remembering. It was all so blurred, so unreal, but after they had finished with Buchanan, after they had kicked and clubbed him beyond humanity, he had thought he recognized that hard and unconquerable face. Then they had turned to him, and the last he remembered was a wheezing voice, a vicious voice that shouted, "Keep him alive. Keep him alive for the rope!"

"My sister will recover," Juan said quietly.

"What made you think it was this Agry did it?"

"Maria told me," Juan said and Buchanan knew what the scratches on Roy Agry's face had reminded him of. It appealed to his ironic sense of humor that he might have killed the buck himself and felt remorse. Seeing the girl again as he had come upon her, abused, naked and near death, he hoped that Agry had been sober enough to know he was paying his bill.

"You shouldn't have gunshot him," Buchanan said.

"I would do it again," Juan answered with some heat. "I wouldn't change anything. Except your trouble."

"I mean it was too honest for a bastard like that," Buchanan said. "It was too easy," he added thoughtfully.

"What would you have done, Buchanan?"

Buchanan — old, thirty-year-old Buchanan — closed his eyes, ran his hands up along the sides of his unshaven face and dreamed he was lying full length in a trough of steaming hot water.

"What would you have done to Roy Agry?" Juan asked again.

"Johnny," Buchanan said, "there are some things that are only for the doing. Not the talking."

"Then in your eyes I managed this business badly?"

"Well, hell! You came all by your lonesome, didn't you? The least you could of done was to bring somebody with you, boy. Somebody like that Gomez would have filled the bill."

"No," Juan said. "It was against my father's orders that I rode at all."

"How come?"

"It is a family thing," Juan said. "My sister is to be married in the spring. Sebastian Diaz is — particular about a great many things. My parents thought it best to postpone justice until after the marriage."

45

"Then kind of ease Mr. Agry out when nobody's looking?"

"Yes."

"But you lean more to Texas law?"

"Once I knew it was Roy Agry, a man who had courted Maria within our own house —"

"You and me both, Johnny," Buchanan said, slapping the younger man's knee reassuringly. "Man, I sure wish you'd brought the makings. I could smoke up a storm." He got up then and began pacing about the little cell restlessly.

CHAPTER SIX

THE new sun had just risen over the hills to the east when a worried and saddle-weary Gomez returned to the hacienda from Agrytown. He knew there could be no delay, and on his instructions Don Pedro was roused.

"I will speak briefly," the segundo told the *patrón* when they were in the study. "A very bad thing has occurred during the night." Immediately Don Pedro stiffened in his chair and his face became a mask. "The young señor," Gomez went on, "traveled across the border into Agrytown. There he sought out the son of Señor Simon and killed him with a gun —"

"Dios mio," Don Pedro whispered involuntarily.

"He was captured, señor, beaten and placed in the jail. I have all this of my own knowledge. Also that Juan is to be tried this morning with Señor Simon Agry as the judge and his brother, the sheriff, as the prosecutor."

"But why, Gomez? What is the reason behind all this?"

"That I cannot say for a certainty, Don Pedro. But just before Juan left the hacienda he was in the room with his sister. Tia Rosa tells me that Maria had regained consciousness and was talking."

47

"I see. Then it was the son of Simon Agry."

Gomez nodded. "I respectfully suggest," he said, "that I lead a force to Agrytown immediately —"

"No. It would fail as it failed in the matter of the stolen horses a year ago."

"But, señor! They will hang the boy. It cannot be!"

Don Pedro's voice dripped ice. "You are raising your voice, Gomez. It is offensive to me."

"A thousand pardons," Gomez snapped, his first display of anger in Don Pedro's presence in forty-three years' association.

"You will wait outside," the *patrón* commanded. "This is a thing that must be solved by deliberation, not emotion."

Gomez swung around abruptly and strode on his short, chunky legs to the door.

"I will summon you," Don Pedro said.

"I will be waiting," Gomez replied.

The summons came an hour later. During that time Doña Isabel had been awakened by her husband and they had held a private conference. Gomez was sent for.

"We have decided to purchase our son's freedom from Señor Simon," Don Pedro announced.

"Purchase?"

"Exactly. At the moment it is most likely that he does not know the circumstances of the case, the mitigating factors. He therefore thinks only of exacting vengeance on Juan and my name."

48

"And that vengeance will be swift," Gomez warned anxiously.

"This was an important decision. It could not be hurried. You will now proceed to Agrytown, alone, and arrange payment of the ransom."

"Alone? But suppose Simon Agry refuses?"

"If my wife and myself have judged the man accurately," Don Pedro said, "then our offer will be accepted. Señor Simon, we believe, puts material things above all else."

"And what is your offer?"

"Gomez," he said, "the negotiations are completely in your hands. You, I am sure, know far better what the financial situation is here than we do. Go now, bring back our son."

"*Sí.*" Gomez bowed to them both and turned to the door.

"Old friend," Don Pedro called in a strangely soft voice. Gomez turned back. "Old friend," Don Pedro said, "do not haggle over the matter. We have no treasure worth the lives of Juan and Maria."

It was, by Agrytown standards, a rather formal trial. The brothers Agry had discussed the procedure at some length during the hours following the shooting, and it was a curious fact that Lew — the uncle rather than the father of the slain man, as well as chief law enforcement agent — was all for hanging both Juan del Cuervo and his accomplice, Buchanan, and then trying them in absentia, as it were.

But Simon prevailed. Mexican or not, enemy

of California or not, Don Pedro del Cuervo still meant something in this whole region. Simon also pointed out that when he was attending to his senatorial duties in far-off Washington he did not want some political rival back here to raise the cry of "lynch law." Not only did he insist upon a trial but Simon wanted a jury that was fairly chosen and not beholden to the Agrys.

The sheriff agreed. What else could he do? In the morning the saloon was swept out, the rows of bottles discreetly covered with burlap, a platform was made out of crates to serve as a bench, and the place was made to resemble a courtroom as nearly as possible. The news that there was actually going to be a hanging *and* a trial caused so much interest that seats inside the place were soon at a premium. Deputy Waldo Peek, acting as bailiff to the court, showed the results of Lew Agry's training by instituting an admission charge of one dollar, first come, first served. And from among the spectators who were also freeholders a jury was empaneled and sworn in by His Honor, Judge Simon Agry.

The judge looked exceedingly stern in his black woolen suit and black foulard cravat — stern but dry-eyed, for in all truth Simon did not feel the stunning loss that another father might. The boy Roy had always been a problem to him, a cause of worry and annoyance rather than filial pride. In adolescence he had been incorrigible, turning not to deeds of simple and forgivable mischief but to downright meanness and willful destruction. Simon had whipped him, whipped him brutally, but that only seemed to goad his peculiar son into fresh acts of vandalism.

Manhood had brought no improvement. Roy had turned sly and mysterious in his comings and goings, sleeping off his liquor by day, doing God-knew-what by night, and apparently content to contribute nothing but his physical presence as the son of the man who owned Agrytown.

And with irritating frequency during the past two years, stories had come back to Simon about Roy's rakehelling with women, far and wide, and not caring particularly whether he was trespassing with some other man's wife or maiden daughter.

Simon Agry rang up a total on his son and found him a liability, both now and in the important future that Simon saw for himself. But, fate had stepped in, fate that had befriended Simon from the day he had hit this country in his desperate escape from Kentucky law. It had been Mexican country then, and so safe that when the war started he had actively helped the federal government. But the handwriting was on the wall, America had a destiny to fulfill, and Simon's adroit switch had left him looking like a patriot all the time. He ended up with Agry County and the money to quiet the embezzling charges still outstanding in Kentucky.

Although the man had no feelings about the death of Roy Agry, he certainly felt something about the incident itself. What he felt was outrage and insult, for if the son of Simon Agry wasn't safe from attack in Simon Agry's town, then who the hell was? He'd set that little matter straight with a vengeance.

There was a stirring in the room and the judge looked up from his harsh thoughts to see that the prisoners were being led to the bar. These two had been arrested by Lew, all right. God, the big one might have been caught in a stampede from the sight of his face. And he favored that right side, Simon knew, because the ribs were cracked.

A thin smile touched the corner of his mouth at the appearance of Don Pedro's precious son. Simon had been one of the two hundred guests at the gala christening for Juan del Cuervo. The gifts had filled the *rancho,* the imported wines had poured like river water, and the fiesta lasted a week. And all for what? So that the kid could grow up and put on enough weight to have his neck broken at the end of a rope.

"This here court's in session!" Waldo Peek bawled raucously. "You two sons gonna plead guilty?"

Simon Agry brought his gavel down sharply. "The bailiff will shut up and sit down somewhere," he said. "Now, then. Which of you two is known as Buchanan? Step forward."

Buchanan, manacled ankle and wrist to Juan, couldn't step forward independently. He presented himself to the court with a half-hearted wave of his free arm.

"Where do you hail from, Buchanan?" Simon asked him.

"West Texas, U.S.A., Judge."

"And where you headed?"

"North."

"What's your occupation?"

Buchanan didn't answer at once.

"Well?"

"I'm trying to think, Judge."

"That seems to be quite a chore for you," Simon said, and the courtroom laughed appreciatively. Even Buchanan smiled, though it hurt like hell to disturb that raw skin on his cheeks.

"I'm not a thinker, Judge," he said agreeably. "But I grew up chasin' cows."

"Whose cows?"

"My dad's," Buchanan said, "till the drought and the bank wiped us out. Then I ramrodded a while for a little border spread. Damn rustlers picked the outfit clean, though. I crossed the border after that and tried to stake myself to a herd of my own."

"By rustling?" Simon Agry asked sarcastically.

"Why, no sir. By fighting."

"Oh! You're a fighter, are you? What kind of fighting?"

"Most every kind there is," Buchanan said. "Providing there's money in it. I kept drifting further west until I met up with a Mex general in Sonora —"

"Campos?"

"The same. You know him, Judge?"

53

"Just by his black reputation," Simon Agry said piously, naturally adding nothing about his gun-running partnership with the bandit.

"And now I'm here," Buchanan said. "So I'm not sure what my occupation is." There was more laughter, but Simon's gavel shut it off quickly.

"You're charged with being an accessory to the murder of Roy Agry," Simon said. "How do you plead?"

"His getting shot was none of my business," Buchanan said. Simon glanced toward his brother Lew.

"You got some questions, Sheriff?"

"Yeah." Lew Agry came and stood squarely in front of Buchanan, their eyes almost on a level. "Mister," he said, "wouldn't you really say you made a living as a gunman?"

Buchanan had been deferential to the judge of this court of law. Now, with a slight squaring of his shoulders, he shed that submissive air and a hard light shone in his pale green eyes. His fingers worked themselves back and forth into fists.

"I've turned a dollar with a gun," he answered, his voice deceptively mild.

"And you've put in a lot of jail time?"

"I've been in jail."

"So the fact is, you're just another hardcase on the dodge?"

"In a way. But I owe the law nothing in the States."

"What about the law in Agrytown?"

"I told the judge how I stand on that charge."

"And I heard. Now tell the judge about the fight you picked with Roy before he was shot."

"Nothing to tell."

"You didn't knock him down?"

"That was no fight. I picked him right up —"

"And got him drunk?"

"He was a man full-grown," Buchanan said. "I offered him a drink and he wanted the whole bottle. He was still working on it when I went across to the hotel and turned in."

"Isn't the fact of the case," Lew Agry said, "that you were the advance agent in this killing? Weren't you sent into town ahead to either goad Roy into a gunfight or get him so drunk he couldn't defend himself?"

"No," Buchanan said simply, with no elaboration or anger.

"But the plan misfired, didn't it? You two pulled off the killing, all right. You got that done. But Del Cuervo ran smack into the law, didn't he? And you come out of your hiding place and tried to break him free, didn't you?" The questions had come hard and fast and Buchanan let the echo of Agry's loud voice die away before he answered.

"The gun shots woke me out of a sleep," he said. "I looked out the window to see this kid here taking a bad licking from that ape over there." He looked at Waldo Peek and drew his glance away with an obvious effort. "So I dealt myself a hand," Buchanan finished, "and landed here."

"You always sleep with your boots on, mister?"

"In this town I do. I wouldn't want to buy 'em back for ten dollars each boot."

"You don't like this town?"

"I don't like several of its citizens."

"Me included?"

"You especially. And him." He looked again at Peek, who grinned and spat on the sawdust floor contemptously.

"You'd like to kill me, would you?" Agry asked.

"I'd like to give you just what you give me, man."

"Take the law into your own hands, that it?"

"Not the law. You."

Agry turned from him and stalked toward the wide-eyed men in the jury chairs. Every one of them would have shelled out good money to see the fight this prisoner wanted with Lew Agry.

"That's the case against this ranny," the sheriff-prosecutor told them arrogantly. "He's a gunman and a Mex lover. He came into town last night by way of the Del Cuervo ranch. He came to kill an Agry because the Del Cuervos are still fighting the war they lost. Those dirty Mexicans hate us all. They're dreaming day and night of marching back into California, knifing and back-shooting every man of us and having our womenfolk." Agry paused and walked slowly along the line, looking intently into each face. "I'm the law in this county," he said meaningfully, letting it sink in. "I arrested this killer in the act of cheating justice. I want a verdict of guilty so's we can hang him as a lesson to every other Mex lovin' son of a bitch around."

There was a frightened silence in the room for many long moments after Lew Agry had walked back to his seat. Someone near the saloon doors clapped, but no one picked it up. From the bench, Simon Agry had been studying his brother's performance with close attention. Lew bore careful studying. He was smart, he was ruthless, and he never did anything without a good reason. What was the reason for such dramatics to hang this Buchanan? He wouldn't have thought the man worth it.

And Simon also remembered Lew's word and the tone of his voice when he said, "I'm the law in this county." Lew needed a little dressing down, a little head shrinking before he stepped too far out of line, and Carbo had to cut him down for good and all.

"Sheriff," Judge Simon Agry said, "I notice that this prisoner has no legal representation."

"He's getting a trial, isn't he?" Lew Agry said, his surprise showing on his face. "What's he need a lawyer for?"

"You don't seem to know too much about the law that you claim to be," his brother said. "California's a new state, but it's run under the same Constitution that governs all the others. You've heard of the Constitution, haven't you, Sheriff?"

Lew Agry rose to his feet, glowering, saying nothing. It was as though he were fighting a battle to say nothing to the man on the bench above him.

"This prisoner's guaranteed due process of the law," Simon said. "I aim to see he gets it."

"What do you mean?"

"I mean you don't have a case, Sheriff." The brothers locked glances, held them, and after a moment that seemed suspended somewhere in time, Lew Agry looked away.

"You don't have a case," Simon repeated, rubbing Lew's nose in it. He rapped the gavel. "Buchanan, you're not guilty, by a directed verdict of this court. Collect your belongings and vamoose."

"Thanks for the kind words, Judge," Buchanan said. "If it's not asking for too much, though, I'd like to put in something else."

"I wouldn't press my luck if I were you," Simon said, his tone blunt and dismissive.

Buchanan didn't seem to notice. "I know, Judge, that it was your flesh and blood that was killed in this saloon last night —"

"This case isn't being judged on any personal bias," Simon said sternly. "This court is neutral. Justice is blind."

"Yes, sir. But this kid here had his reasons —"

"No! *Por Dios,* no!" Juan cried and Buchanan looked at him in vast wonder.

"What do you mean?" he asked in Spanish.

"You are free, Buchanan," came the answer

in the same language. "Go. But say nothing about me. *Nada!*"

"You have to give yourself a chance, hombre! You have to tell these people how it was."

"Never! These people would not agree it was just cause. But that is only a part of it. Do you not understand, amigo, that it is not possible to disclose my reason? My own life is not worth my sister's happiness. I ask you, as a man, to let me decide this thing for myself."

Buchanan shrugged, turned back to find Simon Agry staring at Juan strangely. He guessed then that the judge knew Spanish and understood the facts. Buchanan couldn't make up his mind about this man — he looked one thing and acted another — but he couldn't suppress the feeling of confidence he had that Juan, too, would be freed now that Agry had heard about his son. That feeling was short-lived.

"You are Juan del Cuervo?" Simon asked brusquely.

"As you know."

"You will address this court with respect, Mex!" Simon roared at him, startling the entire room with the unexpected vehemence.

"I am Juan del Cuervo," the young man said.

"You stand charged with the unprovoked murder of one Roy Agry," Simon said. "You are accused of drawing a gun against Roy Agry, and without insult or bodily harm being done to you, of shooting Roy Agry until he was dead. How do you plead?"

"I killed your son, Señor Simon," Juan said.

"Without cause?"

"I hated him," Juan said.

Agry's only betrayal of his knowledge, that Buchanan could see, was an ugly tightening of his massive jawline.

"Then your formal plea is guilty?"

"It is as I said."

Simon's head swung to the jurors.

"You heard the prisoner. He confesses that he killed Roy Agry for no reason but that he hated him. For the record of this trial I want the jury to vote whether they believe his confession or don't believe it. Take the vote."

The jurors looked at each other in puzzlement. Did they believe that the Mex boy had killed Simon's son? Is that what Agry wanted them to vote on?

"What's your verdict?" Simon asked the foreman. That one stood up, glanced at the eleven heads and spoke.

"He did it, all right," he said. "When's the hanging?"

Simon stared down at Juan.

"You've been found guilty of murder by a jury of twelve freeholders of Agry County, California. At an hour before sunset this day you'll be taken to a place of the high sheriff's choosing and hung by the neck until you're dead." Simon raised the gavel. Buchanan's voice intervened.

"Don't he get a chance to say a last word? How about a visit from his family?"

"Mister, don't try the patience of this court —"

"The boy ought to get to say good-by," Buchanan went on insistently. "He's got folks who love him. He's got a sister —"

"No!" Juan shouted brokenly. "No! I do not want them. Hang me now!"

In the midst of that scene at the bench, the saloon doors parted and another Mexican entered the courtroom. The short, solid old man was unarmed, but there was something about the set of him that made every other man in the place move a hand defensively toward his own weapon.

"Gomez! Get out of here. I do not want you!" Juan called.

Gomez did not even glance at Juan, nor at Buchanan, who seemed to have a special talent for getting underfoot. He ignored them both and addressed himself to Simon Agry.

"Señor," he said, "I would speak to you in private."

Lew Agry, who had moved to intercept the intruder, now grabbed him roughly by the arm.

"What kind of trick is this, Mex? How many men you brought with you?"

"I am alone," Gomez said, still talking to Simon. "Will you hear what I have to say?"

"Don't listen to him, Si," the sheriff said, ignoring the dignity of the court. "He's trying to make a deal."

Simon's eyes were speculative. "Take your prisoner, Sheriff," he said and brought the gavel down twice. "Court's adjourned!"

61

Lew Agry and Waldo Peek led both men away, still bound together, and Gomez moved as though to block them.

"Come back to my office," Simon ordered sharply, his voice carrying to Gomez and no farther. "And you'd better have something to say!" Simon climbed down from the table set atop the crates and made his way toward the room he kept for private parties in the rear of the saloon. Gomez followed him inside and closed the door, watching as Agry poured himself a drink from the bottle on the desk. All the way back to Agrytown Gomez had worried about Don Pedro's idea of ransoming Juan. It was not a sound plan for the very simple reason that his *patrón* had very little to offer Simon Agry that would be impressive.

Oh, Don Pedro was comfortably fixed. His family would never miss a meal or be unable to stage a fiesta for their numerous days of celebration. But the principal source of the man's money, in these days of postwar depression for a humbled Mexico, was the proceeds from his estates in far-off Spain. These monies came in irregularly, roughly semiannually, and for the past two years the segundo had made them do almost exclusively for the maintenance of the vast ranch and Don Pedro's two expensive households.

But ransom was an immediate thing. In exchange for one item you gave over another item, in lump sum. Don Pedro had no such emergency fund, neither in cash, horses nor cattle. And even if he pledged the don's solemn word to the contract, Gomez knew that Simon Agry would scoff at any ransom paid in installments. Agry judged all men by his own standards, and by his standards Don Pedro would be a fool to keep on paying for Juan's safe return once that return was an accomplished fact.

So he watched Simon pour himself a drink and another idea came to him, one he had only wishfully considered on the ride from the ranch. It would be a trade — Simon Agry for Juan del Cuervo. But first Agry would have to be as firmly in his possession as Juan was in theirs. And before even considering that, and out of loyal obedience to Don Pedro, he must make an honest effort at bargaining.

"What's on your mind, Gomez?" Simon asked him gruffly. He knew Del Cuervo's man from the old times, the old, desperate times when the Rancho del Rey's foreman had made it a dangerous and frustrating pastime to rustle Don Pedro's stock. All that vast range, all that beef the invading American army needed — and always Gomez outthinking him, waiting for him. In damp weather Simon's hip still ached from the wound inflicted the night he had personally led the raid.

"I have come to purchase the freedom of Don Pedro's son," Gomez said.

"Impossible," Simon said, lowering himself heavily into the chair before the desk. "A jury has convicted him of murder. Of murdering my son."

"Then my mission," Gomez said, "is in vain. I will return to Don Pedro and tell him his fabulous offer has been rejected."

"How fabulous?"

Gomez edged slightly closer. He guessed that Simon was not armed. He guessed, also, that there would be a gun in the drawer of the desk.

"What would you want from Don Pedro?" he asked.

Simon Agry had a fairly good idea of the Del Cuervo finances, but when he spoke his face was bland.

"Twenty thousand American dollars," he said.

"For gold, señor, Don Pedro is hard pressed." Gomez was close enough to the desk now to touch it. He kept his hands relaxed at his side.

"Two hundred horses then," Simon said. "Blooded stock."

"As you know, señor, many horses were stolen from Don Pedro only a year ago. It will be some time before we have two hundred thoroughbreds again." One hard shove, Gomez thought, and then to capture the weapon in the drawer.

"No cash, no horses," Agry said. "In that case I'll accept the deed to Rancho del Rey —"

The door suddenly opened at Gomez' back. He swung around to see Simon Agry's gunman standing there, threateningly.

"Glad you're here, Abe," Agry said to Carbo. "I'll need a witness to a little transaction."

Carbo's cold gaze never left the Mexican's face.

His eyes seemed to be inviting Gomez to do something hostile.

"Is it a deal?" Agry asked.

"Surely, señor," Gomez said wearily, "you are not serious."

"Me? It was you who came here with your fabulous offer."

"I had in mind something more reasonable," Gomez said. "I was prepared to offer you some choice objects from Doña Isabel's jewelry, some priceless family heirlooms —"

"Priceless is right. I'm a businessman, Gomez, not a collector of Spanish junk. The old man can hand over his ranch or bury his son."

"You are a very difficult man, Señor Simon."

"Am I? I'm also a father who's lost his son."

"Have you considered why Juan del Cuervo should have done such a thing to Roy?"

"Juan confessed to murder. What's more, a jury convicted him. He's sentenced to hang, and by hell, it was done fairly, in open court."

"I think you suspect," Gomez said, "that Juan may have been justified."

"I suspect nothing! Now take my offer or reject it."

"I have no authority for such a thing."

"The hell you haven't. You're majordomo, mister. Del Cuervo will back your word the same as he would his own."

Gomez shrugged.

"Well?" Agry growled at him. "Is it a bargain or not?"

"It is a bargain, señor. But the necessary papers are in the vault in Mexicali. It will take several days."

"You've got forty-eight hours, Gomez."

"You will inform the sheriff of the postponement? Your brother will have his heart set on a hanging."

"I'll take care of Lew. You worry about getting back here in time."

Gomez turned and left the room, walking as if he had been stunned. From the first he had known Don Pedro's decision to ransom Juan was a perilous mistake. The don had gauged Simon Agry to be a venal man, but he had badly underestimated how ruthlessly and unreasonably greedy he was. As he mounted and rode out of Agrytown the things that had been said in the office had an aftereffect of nightmarish unreality about them. It was not conceivable that the pig of a Simon Agry was to become the owner of Rancho del Rey. Not conceivable, but a fact none the less.

God had indeed visited them all with a succession of terrible disasters.

CHAPTER SEVEN

FOR his own good reasons, Sheriff Lew Agry paraded the free man and the condemned man through the town square to the jail in their shackles. Moreover, two other deputies joined the processional, bleak-eyed warriors cradling rifles in their arms; rifles that tended to cover Buchanan rather than the supposedly more desperate Juan.

Buchanan knew why, and the sheriff knew that he knew, for he studiously kept himself at a distance from the other man. Then they were back in the jail, in a kind of anteroom, and under the watchful attention of the riflemen Waldo Peek removed the uncomfortable chains.

"Put the Mex in his cell," Agry ordered, and Juan turned to Buchanan.

"*Vaya con Dios,* my friend," he said.

"Yeah," Buchanan said, looking into the boy's pale face.

"It was an honor to know you," Juan said.

"Sure. Honor to know you, too, kid." He rubbed his face. "They say if you get yourself drunk you never feel a thing."

"I will consider your advice, Buchanan," Juan told him.

Waldo Peek took him away. Then men in the anteroom could hear the oaken door slam shut, could hear the bolt slide home. They could also hear the sound of their own breathing. Peek returned, took up a position to one side of Buchanan that completed the ring around him.

"There's a horse out back," Lew Agry said into the silence. "You'll be escorted north a ways."

"A horse?"

"Yours has been confiscated by the state militia."

"I hope he throws you."

"Nothing throws me."

"Except your big brother. And then he stomps all over you."

Lew Agry said, "Waldo," and Peek belted Buchanan in the mouth. The big man's arm cocked to swing back and a rifle barrel slammed down on his wrist.

"Ask for it, mister, and you're sure gonna get it," Lew Agry said. "It'll be like last night was a picnic."

"Go, Buchanan," came Juan's voice anxiously from the cell. "For God's sake, amigo, you cannot stand another beating!"

"All right," Buchanan said to Agry. "I got a horse. I also had a rifle and two Colt handguns."

"State militia," Agry said.

Buchanan's great chest heaved and he took a deep breath.

"And now we come to it," he said. "I want my gold."

"What gold?"

"The purse," Buchanan said very patiently. "The purse with ten thousand gold dollars."

Waldo Peek looked sharply at Lew Agry. Behind Buchanan the riflemen stirred.

"Don't get sucked in, Waldo," Lew Agry said, his voice tight. "You couldn't get ten thousand in that purse."

"Who counted it, Waldo?" Buchanan asked.

"You like to get worked on, don't you?" Lew Agry asked. "You really like it."

"Please, Buchanan, go!" Juan shouted again. "See my father. He will give you money!"

"Don't worry about me, Johnny," Buchanan called back. "I'm going."

"But not south," Agry said. "North."

If Buchanan knew one thing it was that he would have to get away from this hombre very soon or do something suicidal. He didn't know that he could feel this much hate for a man, this much black desire to hurt and keep hurting.

He turned from Agry and his thoughts, brushing the rifle aside negligently as he strode to the door. He opened it and paused for a moment. "So long, Johnny," he called, not looking back. His escort followed him out to the back of the jail, where a sorry excuse for a horse awaited him. He threw a leg over the cracked, mildewed saddle and when the other two were mounted they headed away from Agrytown.

They rode in complete silence, with the guards hanging to the rear, their manner almost deferential. They had seen Buchanan beaten by Lew Agry, beaten and robbed and humiliated. But they had also witnessed the raw clash of personalities, of character, and out of that Buchanan had earned their hard, unspoken respect.

Even had he known, Tom Buchanan couldn't have cared less. Nothing that they could have thought of him, nothing they could have said to him would have mattered. His bitterness numbed him, his disillusionment all but choked him. The homecoming he had dreamed about for two long years, the return of the prodigal; what the hell was this to come home to? Were these who raped, bullied and cheated, his fellow Americans, his brothers? It was hard to take, hard to have the dream shattered so completely.

The trio rode on in silence, and when his escorts realized that Buchanan was oblivious to both the time consumed in the saddle and the jarring gait of his short-winded horse, one of them came forward and touched his arm.

"What do you say to a smoke, friend?"

Buchanan said nothing, only pulled off the trail toward a shaded area, dismounted listlessly and lay full length on the ground. Agry's deputies followed him there, climbed down gratefully and sat with their backs braced against two trees.

"Make one for you?" asked the one who had suggested the break in the journey.

Buchanan shut his eyes. Tobacco, he thought. How he dearly loved a smoke. How he had missed it all these long hours. "No," he said. "Make your own."

"Sorry I asked."

"Go to hell."

Silence.

Then: "Here, Buchanan." A rough-rolled *cigarillo* was pushed between his lips, lit from the one the deputy already had smoking.

Another silence.

"Thanks," Buchanan said.

"I figured you for a smoking man," the deputy said. "Saw how your fingers was stained."

"You packed this one real good."

"Glad you think so."

"Like it fine. How much farther you taking me?"

"To the river. Couple more hours."

"Gonna kill me there?"

"Supposed to."

Buchanan took a deep drag, exhaled the smoke luxuriantly. "Why not here?" he asked.

"Lew wants you out of his county."

"Scared of his brother," Buchanan said.

"Scared of you, too. Funny I never figured Lew Agry to be scared of anything."

"People fool you."

"Yeah. Guess we better get going, Buchanan."

"Be obliged to have it done here, Deputy. That's a misbegotten animal I'm forking."

"Lew wants us to shoot him at the river, too," the deputy said.

They rode on, but now there was a change

in the formation. The one who had provided him with tobacco rode abreast of Buchanan, stirrup to stirrup. His partner, however, held back. An hour later they pulled up again, this time for a meal of cold salted meat and brown bread. It was washed down with a leather sack of red Mexican wine that was passed around from man to man, and topped off by another smoke.

"Was there really ten thousand in your poke?" the deputy asked, breaking the silence at last.

"Nope."

"Five?"

"About. What was your cut?"

"Agry give us each a fifty-dollar piece. Fifty more when we get back."

"Fair enough," Buchanan said with a mocking smile. "Lew supplies the brains."

"So he keeps reminding us. How'd you get that stake?"

"Helping one Mex fight another Mex."

"They tell me that's hard work."

"They didn't tell you the half of it."

The other deputy spoke for the first time. "Let's ride," he said disagreeably, and they began the last stage of the trip to the river. Buchanan held no personal grudge against his guards and suspected that they were just as neutral toward him. This was a rough country, and though there were certain hard and fast rules of conduct there was not yet the same degree of importance about life and death that existed in gentler, more highly civilized regions. And though Buchanan's predicament could be laid directly to the sheriff of Agry-town, the general consensus would be that his luck simply ran out.

But regardless of the time, place or circumstance, a man still carried a strong will to survive. It's his instinct, and now the feeling of resignation with which Buchanan had begun this ride was giving way with each passing mile to a kind of angry regret. He began to think of the good things in this life — of tobacco, of the girls in San Javier, of the lifelong friendships that are made during a roundup. He recalled the deputy making that smoke for him and camaraderie welled up in his chest.

At that moment the deputy drew alongside and touched his arm. "I been parleyin' with my partner about you," he said glumly. "I'm all for leavin' you at the river and just shootin' the horse. But Lafe's too worried about Lew Agry, and he's got a girl back in town and all. Just wanted you to know, Buchanan."

"Thanks, friend. Mighty white of you."

"Wish it could be better tidings," the deputy said and dropped back again.

The river appeared up ahead, quite abruptly. The main trail veered off to the right, making a crossing, Buchanan guessed, at some narrower place. A side trail led left and down the embankment, and now the friendly deputy put his horse ahead of Buchanan's and all three went to the left. The trail began to narrow very soon, with heavy growth on either side. The pace slowed to a walk and Buchanan was conscious of almost nothing else but Lafe's rifle trained on his back.

And what was he going to do about it? Even if he had an alert horse under him there was no possible room to maneuver. He was in a box, and all that remained was for Lafe to close the lid.

"Far enough," the surly voice from behind told him. "Get down slow, mister."

Buchanan swung to the ground, stood looking into the chill, emotionless face of the man on horseback.

"You'll die easier on your knees," Lafe said.

"How would you know how I'll die?"

With a shrug, Lafe primed the rifle.

"No, God damn it — no!" the other deputy cried out, the words sounding wrenched from him. Lafe looked up briefly to find himself in his partner's own gun sights.

"Don't fight me, Pecos."

"Lafe, I got no other choice. Now set that weapon down and let's talk on it some more."

"Talk, hell!" Lafe said, and his agitation gave Buchanan the only chance he had. He moved and the gun roared down at him. The second gun fired in practically that same moment and the slug lifted Lafe bodily out of the saddle. The stirrups held and he toppled lifelessly forward across his horse's neck. The spooked animal tried to throw off the unnatural rider but Buchanan steadied it with a firm jerk of the reins.

Pecos came up on foot, and between them they got Lafe to the ground and laid him out. Buchanan tore the already bloodsoaked shirt front away, and beside him Pecos groaned.

"Godamighty," he said with sorrow. "Clean through the heart."

Buchanan moved away, saying nothing. This was a delicate moment, a private moment, and he was the intruder. He was also the reason that the man's partner was dead, and because Pecos seemed to be an unpredictable type, Buchanan prudently retrieved the fallen rifle and awaited developments.

But he had overrated the friendship between the two, for Pecos recovered from his bereavement with a very practical question.

"What in hell am I gonna do now?" he asked.

"You got anything holding you in Agrytown?"

"Just a bill at Simon's saloon."

"Then why not pick up some of that gold dust up north a ways?"

"You goin' there?"

"That's my destination," Buchanan said.

"Prospectin's expensive, hear them tell about it."

"Yeah."

Buchanan's glance wandered idly to the dead body of Lafe. When he looked back at Pecos he found his own idea kindling in the other man's face.

"Why not?" Pecos asked softly. "Lew Agry ain't God."

"You'll do, Pecos," Buchanan told him warmly. "Let's ride."

"Could we first say a few words over Lafe here?"

There were no tools with which to dig a grave so they carried the man into the deep foliage and covered him with leaves and branches. Pecos doffed his slouch hat, revealing himself to be a much younger man than Buchanan had thought, and spoke in a clear, forthright voice.

"Lafe, you and me worked for Lew Agry near onto a year, though I don't guess we were ever buddies. But I'm sorry it was me that stopped your clock. You had your good side, Lafe, like us all, and you could be mean when the liquor was in you. Nobody's gonna hold that against you. I'm even callin' it bygones about your everlastin' cheatin' at stud and for stealin' that Spanish saddle the time we raided Don Pedro. I guess," Pecos said, "that the reason we never cottoned up was your bein' part Apache and me bein' all Texan. Well, Lafe, I got me a West Texan for a partner now and when it came to choosin' between you I hope you know I did what I had to do. So long, Lafe. You died real good."

Pecos replaced his hat.

"You put a lot of store in being Texan," Buchanan said casually.

"A man's got to be loyal to where he was born."

"How come you're in California?"

"Fiddle-footed," Pecos answered. "This

76

country's so damn big a man itches to move around in it. One day I got tired of watchin' the sun go west and just followed it out here. Next I'm gonna trail it clear across the ocean."

"The sun'll just lead you back to Texas."

"Where I'll die happy. What do you say we get movin', Buchanan?"

"Sure."

"First take these," Pecos said. He extended his hand and in the palm were two fifty-dollar gold pieces. "Lafe don't need his where he's goin'," he said, "and I don't want nothin' of yours I stole."

Buchanan lifted one of the coins and dropped it into his pocket.

"Fifty-fifty," he said. "Share and share alike."

Chapter Eight

THAT'S a good deal you made, Si," Lew Agry said to his brother. "A real smart deal. For you."

"Your whining," Simon said, "gets harder and harder on my ears. That and your biggedy ideas of your own importance." He flicked a cigar ash on the rug of the sheriff's office.

"This town is growing," Lew said. "I'm trying to keep it from busting the seams."

"You didn't keep Roy from getting killed. With all these new gunmen you're hiring, you didn't stop that."

"I'm not letting his killer off scot-free, neither."

"That's my business."

"Sure, Si. Like I said, you made a good deal out of Roy's getting shot down like some tramp cowboy."

"Speaking of tramps, what became of that other one we tried this morning?"

"I sent him out of town."

"With his goods?"

"I fined him his horse and saddle for disturbing the peace," the sheriff said.

"Amos told me about his leather purse," Simon said. "Nothing smaller than ten-dollar gold pieces."

"News to me."

"My barkeep says the same thing. Buy yourself a new belt, Lew?"

Lew Agry closed his coat over the silver-buckled belt that had once belonged to Tom Buchanan.

"Won it from a fella," he said.

"I hope he's a good loser."

"He is."

"How come you sent this Buchanan out of town under two guns? What were you worried about?"

"Anybody report what I had for breakfast this morning, Si?"

"I thought I made a special point of setting that boy free at the trial," Simon said. "I sure hope you didn't buck me, Lew. That tin star on your chest ain't anyways near permanent, you know."

"Meaning exactly what?"

"That the Lord giveth, and the Lord taketh away," Simon snarled, placing his huge hands on the arms of the chair and pushing himself to his feet. "The hanging's temporarily postponed," he told his brother. "If it's on again you'll hear from me." Abe Carbo pulled the door open and both men left.

When the door had closed, Lew Agry got up himself and strode to the window, stood looking out while Simon boarded the gleaming black surrey he had had freighted especially from Chicago, watched as the shadowlike Carbo mounted his dun and rode point as they traveled out toward Simon's house.

Del Cuervo's land, Lew was thinking. No, it

wasn't possible. By the skin of his teeth Simon had missed the firing squad only a few years back. By being the only promoter on the scene he had staked a claim to what he called Agry County, and somehow made the claim stand up.

Lew knew the Simon Agry story. He'd been there — the bully-boy gunman who'd made the whole country safe for Simon just as Abe Carbo protected him on a trip across the street now. Lew's reward had been a thousand acres, the badge, and the right to scrounge and plunder across the border. But Lew was ambitious, and his ambition showed. He was also contemptuous of Simon's airs, of Simon's calling the shots without ever risking being shot at. And the contempt showed.

But Rancho del Rey — parlaying his son's death into the ownership of that! You could take Agry County and lose it in Don Pedro's land. What was more, Simon would have it legally, whereas in Washington they would eventually get around to pricking the balloon that was Agry County and returning it to the supervision of the state.

And what was Lew's cut? It was the back of Simon's hand, that's what it was. Nor would it stop there. His brother was feeling Lew's restiveness, he was suspiciously aware of the hardcase deputies Lew was hiring, ostensibly to secure Simon's grip on the county, but a group whose first loyalty was to the sheriff. Simon was feeling the pressure and he was considering the ways and means of easing Lew out of the picture. Simon would figure it out to the last detail. It would be another chess puzzle, with Simon playing Abe Carbo as the attacking knight, either in a ruthless assassination, or feinting with the gunman while he maneuvered his other pieces to bring the sheriff down in a bloodless coup.

And during these moments, with the surrey passing from sight down the dusty street, Lew Agry came to his decision. To wait for Simon to move would be to play the other man's game. That was not Lew's way. He was the mover, the man on the prod, and now he saw that if he were ever to get his full partnership with Simon this situation was made to order.

"Waldo?"

"Yeah, Lew," said the dull voice from the corner.

"You afraid of Abe Carbo?"

"No."

"You afraid of my brother?"

"Only if you are, Lew."

"I'm going to spit in his eye."

"He's going to spit back."

"You with me?"

"All the way."

"That's about how far it's going to go. Come night, take Hamp and Ivy over to the jail. Get the Mex kid and ride him out to old Emerson's shanty on the river road."

"Emerson?"

"The old man can hardly move around," Lew Agry said. "Hear he's half blind. Just take some

81

grub and a bottle out to him and he won't know enough to ask questions. It's the last place Simon will look for the kid, and he's only got forty-eight hours to do all his looking."

"With the three of us gone," Peek said, "you won't have nobody much left in town to side you."

"Pecos and Lafe'll be back. You might even meet 'em on the way."

"If so, how about tradin' jobs with Pecos? Rather be here when the trouble starts."

Lew Agry slapped the man on the back.

"One half bull," he said, "and the other half tiger. You just cotton natural to a fight, don't you?"

"I reckon," Waldo said, thinking that what Agry said was partly true. No need to tell the boss how primed he'd been all day to have another go at the Apache girl.

"Sure, Waldo. If you run across the Texan leave him take charge of the kid."

Peek nodded. There wasn't going to be any if about it.

CHAPTER NINE

MY home for my son," Don Pedro said stoically. "So be it, Gomez."

"It was as though I were dealing with *el diablo* himself," Gomez said. "It was not an agreement between two human beings, señor."

"Nevertheless, it will be honored." Don Pedro rose from the high-backed armchair in the candle-lit room and moved slowly to the writing table. He has aged, Gomez thought. The Don walks slowly, almost hesitantly, and he is not ramrod stiff. Off to one side sat Doña Isabel, saying nothing in this moment of crisis, holding a simple black rosary in her deceptively fragile-looking hands. By her very silence she communicated strength, and Gomez, who had asked himself over the years who possessed the greater fortitude of these two aristocrats, now thought he knew.

"It will not be necessary to leave my son in Simon Agry's hands another forty-eight hours," Don Pedro said, setting himself down at the table with a piece of his official paper and pen. "The so-called deed in the vaults at Mexicali is a royal grant. It is not transferable."

"Then Agry cannot hold title?" Gomez asked hopefully.

"He will have this signed paper from me," Don Pedro said, "that will relinquish my claims in his favor. It will be binding on me and my heirs, but I cannot answer for the federal government. I am certain that Simon Agry will find the ways and means."

"Sí," Gomez said worriedly. "He may even use any opposition as an excuse to call the American army. Our country has been invaded for less cause."

"The war is over, Gomez. If our two nationalities cannot live side by side, at least the two governments have had enough of the fighting."

There was only the scratching of the pen on parchment then, as Don Pedro wrote the necessary legal terms. He signed his name very deliberately and added the date.

"Let Ramon take some men and go to Agrytown," he said. "You have ridden far too long this one day."

Gomez shook his iron-gray head stubbornly. "It is my duty, señor. This one time I must insist."

"As you will. And, Gomez — you realize that this is your last mission as major-domo. We are no longer patrón and vaquero. El Rancho del Rey is gone."

Gomez realized that. He had considered the thing so thoroughly that now it was an accepted fact.

"Gomez," Doña Isabel said softly, "you had better leave. I am anxious to see Juan again."

Gomez left the hacienda, signaled to the waiting Ramon and two riders, and all four went back along the road to the border.

Maria del Cuervo heard the urgent sound of the departing horses and sat upright in the bathtub.

"Felice! See what it is!"

The Indian servant had been standing with a warm towel. Now she ran to the window.

"It is Gomez and Ramon, señorita. And two vaqueros. They go like the wind."

"Something important is happening," Maria said. The girl had been told nothing about her brother. She had asked for Juan as soon as the doctor had left this morning, asked for him to verify whether she had dreamed a brief conversation with him or whether it had actually occurred. But she was told Juan was on spring roundup, and though that was a reasonable explanation there was the air of secrecy in Tia Rosa's voice that made her anxious. The entire household was under a strain, for that matter, and it was not wholly connected with what had befallen her.

The doctor, for instance, declared in a very strong voice that she was not injured, that she was strong as a tiger. Her own deep relief, though, had been only partially mirrored in the faces of her parents. Her father and mother had stayed on in the room, reassuring her that everything was going to be all right, strengthening her morale. But when they were gone it came to her that not once had she been asked about Roy Agry. Was it of no importance, then? Maria knew better. So it had to be the other reason. They hadn't asked the name of her attacker because they already knew.

And the comings and goings of Gomez. All through the day he had arrived at the hacienda and departed, always with a clouded face, always with an air of doom.

Felice told her as much as she knew, as much as she could learn herself and from the other servants. Gomez, for instance, had discovered her body — but there was some sort of mystery about that, too.

Maria's eyes had widened.

"You mean — it may have been some other man who came upon me? One of the vaqueros?"

"Señorita," Felice said, "it is the account of the thing that the segundo found you. But my brother Amaya, who rode with the searchers, told me of another man who was carrying you in his arms."

"*What* man?"

"A stranger to my brother, señorita. Amaya describes him as formidable."

Maria shivered. "Formidable?"

"A giant, Amaya says."

"But Amaya is so small."

"Even so, Amaya says he had a fierce look on him."

"But if he — if this stranger rescued me, carried me in his arms . . . How was I dressed, Felice?" she asked quickly.

Felice shook her head, following her mistress's

thinking with a female understanding. "I was not there, señorita."

"I am sure it was Tio Café who found me," Maria announced resolutely. "That is the way of it."

"I am sure, also," Felice agreed.

"And of the other, the one who attacked me? What do they ask about him?"

"Nothing, señorita."

"Nothing? Doesn't my father or my brother care?"

"Of course they care. But the man is known to them. The son of Señor Simon."

"How? How could they know?"

The Indian shrugged her shoulders. "It is just that they know," she explained.

Now Maria had the added puzzle of Gomez rushing from the ranch with three others. Something important was happening, something that was being kept from her. She stood up and stepped from the tub, a flawless figure of a girl with her father's angular face and straight shoulders. She was raven-haired, olive-skinned and surprisingly curved and firm-breasted. Felice wrapped her in the big towel and she stood braced while the Indian's powerful hands dried her vigorously.

She remembered again how she had fought against the insane brutality of Roy Agry. As she had resisted him until he had been forced to beat her unconscious. And today, with the resilience that was her mother's heritage, she bore no more spiritual scar from the incident than when the rattlesnake had attacked her as a child of ten. Gomez — her Tio Café — had been there that time, too, to slit open the wound on her forearm and suck the venom out of the bloodstream.

That had given her a respect for rattlesnakes, and a healthy caution. But she was not afraid to ride among them. Nor was she afraid to ride among men, either. She would just be on guard, that was all. If a Roy Agry met her on the trail she would not treat him with the complete trust that she had. The next man who tried to force her into the brush would find a stiletto in his ribs.

With that thought in her active mind, Maria dressed in one of the dozens of frilly, feminine gowns from her wardrobe. At supper tonight she must try to make her parents more cheerful.

Chapter Ten

THOUGH a priest would have been a comfort to the young man in these last hours, Juan had found peace within himself and with his God by the time they came for him. He was calm when the door was unbolted and thrown open; much more so than Waldo Peek, who had fully expected that he and the two deputies with him would have to drag the youth from his cell. Instead, Juan submitted to having his wrists bound and walked out between the men of his own free will.

Juan did wonder about two things. For one, Señor Simon had set the time of his hanging for an hour before sunset. Why had they waited until now, when it was almost pitch-dark on a moonless night? And he wondered why his guards were so tense, why they led him from the jail so furtively, their hands actually resting on gun butts. Were his father and Gomez planning a desperate rescue? He hoped not, but in any event he must be alert to help if and when the situation presented itself.

He was boosted to the saddle of a strange horse, not the fine animal he had arrived on, and was taken out of town by the back road.

Buchanan and Pecos, riding the same trail from the opposite direction, measured their pace in consideration of how far their mounts had already traveled and what hard riding possibly lay ahead. Their plan was a simple one and had been decided briefly along the way. Pecos would search out Lew Agry, on the natural pretext of reporting Buchanan's death at the river, and then Buchanan himself would make his appearance. Pecos expected opposition, but he doubted very much whether Agry was the man to hold out on Buchanan, all things considered.

"What's that light over there?" Buchanan asked.

"Old man Emerson's place."

"Friend of yours?"

"So-so. Thinkin' about some grub?"

"That," Buchanan said, "and some feed for these horses. Man, we've been pushing right along today."

Pecos nodded and slowed until he found the wagon-wide path that led to the adobe shanty a quarter of a mile away. A hundred feet short of the place he halted, Buchanan beside him.

"Emerson!" he called between his cupped hands. "Hey, old man!"

"Git the hell off my land!" came a mean, crackling voice.

"This is the law!" Pecos shouted back sternly. "Now lay up the rifle. We're comin' in peaceable." Even so, Pecos hesitated.

"Well, come if you're comin'!" called the irascible voice then. The two horsemen guided their mounts carefully toward the house, and moments later Buchanan made out the shaggy-haired form of a small, almost impossibly thin old man who stood in the gathering darkness with an ancient rifle cradled in his arm.

"Which of Lew Agry's thieves be you?" Emerson asked with belligerence.

"I'm Pecos. We met."

"Who's the other?"

"You know Lafe?"

"No."

"Well, this is Lafe then." Pecos dismounted. "We dropped by for a little hospitality, old man."

"Ain't got none to give away."

"In that case we'll either buy it," Pecos said, "or help ourselves. Which will it be?"

"This ain't no mission stop," Emerson said. "You'll pay for what you get."

"Fair enough. We'll provide for the horses and you rustle up some steak and spuds."

"Tonight's menu," Emerson snapped, "is chili and beans. Take it or ride on."

"Heat it up then," Pecos said. He and Buchanan led their mounts to the old Spanish watering trough and then Pecos pitched two piles of dried-out hay. They returned to the little house and squatted on the earthen floor with their bowls of chili.

Campos, Buchanan thought, would have hung this old man by his thumbs for setting out such a flat-tasting mess — but then Campos rarely let such a long time go between meals. Fantastic how that man could endure anything without a murmur — except the slightest pang of hunger. Then you could hear him bellow clear to Chihuahua . . .

"What shenanigans your boss up to these days?" Emerson was asking Pecos.

"Enforcin' the law as usual," Pecos said, and when Emerson cackled derisively the Texan made no comment.

"Those stogies for sale, mister?" Buchanan asked, indicating the black Spanish cigars on the shelf above the fireplace.

"A dollar apiece."

Pecos choked. "Those ropes cost you two for a jit!"

"In Agrytown where I got 'em. The extra is the shippin' charges."

Buchanan strode to the shelf. "I'll take five," he said. "How much for the chili?"

"Five dollars each bowl. Coffee's free."

"Old man," Pecos said, "you've finally gone loco out here all by yourself! You'll take a paper dollar and thank us."

"You agreed to pay my prices —"

"Hold it!" Buchanan said suddenly, his powerful voice commanding an instant silence. Then, from outside, came the sound of someone else calling to the house as Pecos had.

"Who is it?" Buchanan asked.

"Don't know. Go see, Emerson."

The old man's lively eyes danced from one face to the other. Trouble was an ancient acquaintance of his, and from the very tone of their voices he knew that something was not right. He moved to the door and opened it.

"Who's out there?"

"Sheriff's men, Emerson! Don't get trigger happy!"

Emerson grinned at Pecos and Buchanan, toothlessly and maliciously. "Well, now," he said. "Who's the law, and who ain't?"

"Invite 'em in," Pecos said. "But I'd be strictly neutral, old man. Remember, you ain't been paid yet."

"We're comin' in, Emerson!" shouted the voice outside.

"Suit yourself, Deputy." Emerson left the door ajar and removed himself to the corner of the room protected by the chimney. Buchanan placed his back against the wall beside the open door.

"I place the voice as Hamp Horne," Pecos said in a quiet undertone. "Should I parley with him outside?"

Buchanan nodded. "I'll cover you through the door."

Pecos went on out into the night. Immediately there was surprised recognition.

"Pecos! Now what the hell you doin' here?"

"Eatin'. Who you got there, Hamp?"

"Me and Waldo and Ivy brung the Mex kid out to light a spell."

"I figured he'd be hung and buried by now."

"Complications. Seems the kid's old man ransomed him off of Simon. But that left Lew out

93

and now he's in the ransom business his own self."

"Buckin' the big man, is he?"

"Had to come one fine day."

"You say Waldo's along?"

"Yeah. He's on the trail waitin' to meet up with you. Waldo wants to get back to town real bad. He fixed it with Lew that you was to take his place watchin' the kid." Hamp, a lean, nondescript type, dismounted. "Lafe," he said, "can find Waldo and explain that you're already here . . ." His voice trailed off foolishly as he looked beyond Pecos's shoulder to the form of Buchanan filling the doorway.

"Lafe is dead," Pecos said. "That hombre with the gun in his big fist is my new partner."

"What's that supposed to mean to me?" Hamp asked.

"It shouldn't mean nothin', Hamp. Not unless you want it to."

Buchanan could not be sure whether he saw the other deputy make a hostile move, or whether he sensed it. But the Colt jumped twice in his hand and Ivy Storrs twisted in the saddle and plunged headlong to the ground.

"That's enough," Hamp Horne said when the same gun swung his way.

"Drop your belt, then, and march inside."

Horne quickly obeyed.

"What about the kid?" Pecos asked.

Buchanan was already walking to where the wrist-bound Juan sat his horse. From Buchanan's first unbelievable appearance in that doorway to his presence now had consumed too little time for the whole startling sequence to fully register.

"Didn't expect to see you again, Johnny," Buchanan said, unknotting the rope.

"Are we both dead, amigo? Or what?"

"You're both gonna be," Pecos said, "unless we make some plans about Mr. Waldo Peek out there. I've tracked with that one and he ain't human."

Buchanan handed Hamp's discarded gunbelt to Juan. "Might as well borrow the horse, too," he suggested. "That Agry sure don't provide decent transportation for his guests."

A laugh burst joyously from Juan's throat, bubbling up out of him contagiously. Even Pecos grinned at the sound, and realized how long it had been, and how much had intervened, since he himself had felt as unconstrained as that. He was just as quickly sobered by the thought of Peek, alerted by the gunshots and waiting for them in the darkness.

But Waldo wasn't waiting. Hearing the firing from the main trail, he had put it down to a surly greeting from old man Emerson. Then, to head off an unnecessary ruckus, he had located the wagon path and made his way toward the house at full gallop.

He and Buchanan met head-on as he rode into the midst of the group in front of the shack with the impetus of Peek's bigger horse and greater speed driving Buchanan sideways into Pecos and knocking the drawn Colt from Buchanan's hand.

"Hamp, god damn it!" Peek bellowed, and in the same instant recognized Buchanan in the darkness. He fired from a rearing horse, missed, and fired again.

"I'm hit," Pecos groaned at Buchanan's back. Buchanan, weaponless, closed with Peek recklessly. He got his hands on the man's powerful shoulders and launched himself from the stirrups.

"Peek," Buchanan said, low as a whisper, "I'm not going to kill you but when I'm through you'll wish I had."

Peek resisted the first charge, but the momentum of Buchanan's body bore him backward and down. Nearly five hundred pounds of fighting men made the earth around them jar as they hit and rolled over and over, Peek working his knee like a piston. Buchanan immobilizing the wrist that held the gun while his thumb sought Peek's windpipe.

Peek brought his head up in a sudden butt that Buchanan felt to the soles of his feet. Peek sensed his advantage and butted again. But instead of Buchanan's bleeding nose, the target was Buchanan's indestructible forehead, and the advantage was quickly reversed.

Buchanan tossed a leg over Peek, came to his knees in a mounted position. His fists beat down remorselessly on that face below him, watched it change shape, felt the bones snap, stopped hitting only when he was too arm-weary and knuckle-sore to continue. He rolled off Peek's body and lay full length on his back, sucking in great gasps of air.

"Buchanan, can you hear me?"

"Sure, Johnny."

"Your friend has a wound in the stomach. I cannot stop the bleeding."

Buchanan made his way to Pecos's side. Not only was the wound pouring blood, but the Texan was hemorrhaging from his mouth and nostrils.

"He has only minutes to live," Juan said quietly.

"I know. God damn it, kid, I know."

Chapter Eleven

THE sound of the horses pounding in the street outside brought Lew Agry hurrying to his office window. But the tongue-lashing he planned for Pecos and Lafe died aborning. It was not his deputies hurrying past but Gomez and three Del Cuervo vaqueros.

Now what? the sheriff thought irritably. According to Simon it was going to take Gomez forty-eight hours. What was he doing here tonight? Had Don Pedro reneged? Was there a counter offer? He swung back to the desk and poured liquor into his glass. Whatever it was, they'd have to come to Lew Agry. Lew held the trumps this time around.

That thought flowed effortlessly into another, one not so satisfying, and for the tenth time within the last hour he glanced at the wall clock and wondered where his missing men were. And that brought his mind full circle to the big worry: Abe Carbo.

Lew knew he could handle the gunman. If it came to that, he'd take him. He slammed the glass down. But why should it ever have to come to that? What the hell did he have all those deputies for, anyhow? By hell, they'd feel his spurs when they showed up.

Abe Carbo heard the same horsemen five minutes later, heard them turn into the entrance to Simon's house. He was out on the protected veranda in an instant, to see what was going on and to see what Simon called the Home Guard. Not bad, he thought, seeing the dozen guns that both confronted the riders and covered them from the low roofs of the adjacent buildings. Not good, either. These were third-rate fighters at best, a motley collection of drifters and dodgers that he'd had to prime with raw whisky to drive off the Del Cuervo outfit last year.

But they were all that Simon Agry would let him buy. He said he couldn't afford to pay gun wages to a first-class crew. He said he wasn't the governor of California, he was only a private citizen. He said.

The fat man was afraid. Afraid of the past, afraid of the future. Afraid of his brother, of his kid, of Carbo — especially of Abe Carbo, who guarded his life for him. . . .

"Carbo! What's going on out there?" Simon demanded.

"The ambassador from Mexico is calling," Carbo answered with his insolent drawl. "You want to see him?"

Simon stepped heavily onto the veranda.

"What's he doing back here tonight? Who's that with him?"

"I don't know. But the vaqueros are his safe-conduct pass when you turn over the kid." Carbo suddenly laughed. "Look at them."

Gomez and his men pretended to have trouble halting their snorting, high-spirited mounts before the semi-circle of armed men. Almost as one, the four horses reared back on hind legs, scattering the line, then wheeled and came back on all fours with their rumps presented contemptuously to Simon Agry's Home Guard. Gomez alone dismounted, glanced at the riflemen on the roofs, spit at the ground and bore down on the pair waiting on the veranda. The segundo was reliving Agry's horse raid, the galling rout at the border when Don Pedro had not let his vaqueros regroup and redeem themselves. Gomez was mad as a hornet.

"Step back inside, Si," Abe Carbo said, without taking his eyes from the approaching Gomez. "Hold it right there, Mex!" he called out, his voice a crackling warning, the drawl gone.

Gomez halted, feet planted wide apart, challenge in every muscle of his solid little body.

"You come to dicker or fight, hombre?" Carbo asked coldly, but less belligerently. He would accommodate Del Cuervo's envoy with anything he wanted, but he knew that neither he nor Gomez would profit by a meaningless shoot-out. And he seemed to have reached the other man's basic good sense.

"I have come with the ransom for Juan del Cuervo," Gomez said stiffly.

"Come on in then, amigo."

"Is the boy in there?"

"No. He's in the jail."

100

"Then I will deliver the ransom at the jail. Amigo." Gomez turned his back on Carbo and the big house, returned to his horse, remounted, and with a sharp order led his men out of the courtyard.

"What was that all about?" Simon Agry said peevishly, his manner once more important.

"He's just feeling the strain," Carbo said.

"He is, is he?"

"I wouldn't ride him, Si," the gunfighter advised. "And I wouldn't keep him waiting at that jail."

Simon snorted his impatience. "Bring the carriage around," he ordered. Carbo relayed the order, then went among the crew and gave specific riding instructions. Four men immediately mounted and rode out ahead. Four more went singly to take up strategic positions near the sheriff's office, the livery and the hotel. The remainder awaited the surrey and trailed it and Abe Carbo to the jail.

A gaudy show of force, Carbo reflected as they moved along. But if he didn't have quality troops, then he had to make do with quantity and bluff. Give him that pair Lew had, that Pecos and Lafe. Those two and the bull, Waldo. Hell — let him work with that big boy on trial this morning, the one with the quick-looking hands. A rare smile touched Carbo's eyes as he thought of Buchanan and how the two of them could take over this Agry County setup between breakfast and dinner. West Texas, he had said. Well, that was

101

where they grew them.

Carbo knew about all there was to know about that breed. All about Texas, West and East, also New Orleans, Memphis, Pensacola (where he'd been born), Chicago, New York City, and wherever else gambling and gunplay lured a restless man in a restless country.

Carbo was a native son, but his roots and his motivation were European. His father was Gino Carbo, a Sicilian, member of an ancient and legendary family whose only professions had been banditry, kidnaping and hired assassination. Gino Carbo, at seventeen, had come to America for the sole purpose of raising a war chest for his beleaguered kin, then engaged in a disastrous vendetta.

After three years he had none of the needed gold, but enough of the language to court and win a Georgia belle. Their son was named for Gino's father-in-law, Abraham Cooper, and when the boy was six his father was killed in a gunfight. Lily Carbo had no understanding of her fierce-eyed, terrible-tempered son, no hold over him. When he was twelve Abe Carbo had made his way to New Orleans, shipped aboard a river boat, and during the next eight years learned all there was to know about cards and dice, all there was to know about guns and fighting, and how to make that temper work for him and not against him.

By the time he was twenty Abe Carbo already had the reputation of a scrupulously honest gambler, but a killer who looked for and took every advantage. It was a reputation that made others uncomfortable in his presence, that kept Carbo constantly on the move in search of new places, new faces. In the vast land called Texas, this reputation made his guncraft much in demand. He had sold his skill and his nerve in the Territory for a decade. Now, in his fortieth year, he was in California.

And this was where he was going to stay. The boom in the north held no interest at all. He felt uncomfortable now in crowded, bustling gold towns. He had met too many faces to remember them all, had made too many enemies to defend himself against the ambushes and back-shooters. This country, this Agry County, had space and distance. Abe Carbo worked for a fraction of his regular wages because he saw how easily the Agry brothers could be toppled.

Give him Buchanan, and the land would be theirs between breakfast and dinner.

They were passing the sheriff's office, and for a fleeting moment he had glimpsed Lew Agry's face at the window. A strange place for Lew to be when he should be at the jail to make delivery of the prisoner, he thought. Now they wheeled toward the jail building, and Carbo touched spurs to his horse to ride ahead and get the picture. Gomez waited there, impatience in the set of his shoulders, a smoldering look on his face. And a crowd had gathered, a wary Agrytown crowd that wisely stood out of the line of possible fire.

The surrey drew up within ten yards of the waiting Mexicans, and Carbo pulled his horse up close beside it.

"Do your talking from here," Carbo said to Simon, and the man in the carriage looked at him nervously.

"They wouldn't dare try a play here," he said. "Not just the four of them."

"We see four," Carbo said. "But get down if you want to. Gomez won't."

That made it all right. Simon could see the propriety in not having to look up to a man on horseback.

"Let's have the papers, Gomez," he commanded for all to hear.

"Let us first see the boy," Gomez answered.

Simon waved his arm. "Bring the Mex kid out here," he said, and when no one jumped to carry out the command he looked around for particular faces. "Where's the sheriff?" he demanded. "Where's the jailer?" Still no movement, no answer. Abe Carbo raised his hand and the four he had dispatched to the jail emerged from among the onlookers.

"Get Del Cuervo out here," Carbo said. The men went inside the building, stayed there for tantalizing minutes and came back outside. A murmur swept the crowd when there was no Juan del Cuervo with them.

"Gomez?" Carbo called out quickly.

"I hear you."

"Keep your head. We know nothing of this."

"I warned Señor Simon," Gomez said heavily. "He assured me that he could control the sheriff."

"By hell, if Lew is tampering with my plans —"

Carbo shut him off. "We will go together to the sheriff's office," he said to Gomez. The surrey and its guard swung around and proceeded toward Lew Agry's headquarters with the suspicious Del Cuervo contingent following.

Lew Agry watched the ominous cavalcade approach, all alone. Gone from his mind were those hard, clever answers he was going to give his brother. Gone was that sure, firm touch with which he was going to control the situation. Quickly he loosened his gunbelt, put the weapon conspicuously on a wall hook. He put the bottle out of sight, lit a cigar with a hand that trembled expectantly, and planted himself firmly in the chair behind the desk. Wild horses wouldn't drag him out of this office.

The door burst open and Abe Carbo stood there, a mocking smile on his thin lips. Carbo's eyes roamed from Agry's sullen face to the gun on the wall. Then he stepped forward, a signal to Simon, who entered stormily.

"Where is he, Lew?" he roared. "Where's the kid?"

"No need to take the roof off, Si. The kid is safe and sound . . ."

"Where?"

"I was worried about some hotheads, some

friends of Roy's busting in for a lynch party —"

"You liar!"

The sheriff looked hurt. "I don't figure you, Si," he said. "You own a very important piece of property in that kid, but you're content to leave him unprotected."

"Thanks, Lew, from the bottom of my heart. Now, damn it, where is he?"

"Out at Emerson's," the sheriff said.

A dry laugh sounded from Abe Carbo's throat. "Now there's a safe spot," Carbo said.

"What's this got to do with you?"

"Hook that belt back on, Lew, and I'll debate it."

"There'll be time for that, Abe," Simon Agry said. "Let's get to Emerson's pronto!"

Carbo followed the fat man to the door, glanced back once at Lew Agry and was gone. A moment later both parties of horsemen were off for Emerson's place on the river road.

Chapter Twelve

HOLD up, Johnny-boy," Buchanan said. "Company comin'." The oncoming sound had reached his ears over the pounding of their own horses' hoofs, telling Buchanan something of their number and making him cautious. By this time, anything bound out of Agrytown made them jumpy.

"We can leave the trail here," Juan said, spying a bypath. They ducked out of sight and waited, handguns out and ready.

A minute later they made out the solidly packed outline of a dozen horsemen and the silhouette of a surrey. Faces were unrecognizable in that blackness, but the passenger in the carriage could be no one else but Simon Agry. Then Juan cried out.

"What's the matter?"

"It was Gomez, and some others of our riders!"

"You sure?"

"Amigo, my first memory is that of Tio Café in the saddle. It is as if he is part of the horse."

"Then they're off to find you and pay over the ransom. Which makes it twice as important that you ride on straight to your ranch."

"No, Buchanan. It is as I said back there when we covered the face of your friend. My father must see you and hold your hand. It is a thing of great importance."

"And like I told you, kid — me and your country have parted ways. I got one little side trip to make back to Agrytown, and then it's north all the way. Hell, I'm even considerin' a spell at fur trappin'."

"Then I go along. First on the side trip, and then into the fur venture. I cannot replace Pecos, but I will work hard and not complain."

"Johnny, you got a cussed streak in you a yard wide."

"Yours is twice as wide."

Buchanan chuckled. "Maybe because I'm twice as big. Let's ride!"

Buchanan set a faster pace now, and soon the pale glow of Agrytown's lights showed just ahead. Another quarter-mile and the main trail swung left while a narrower, less traveled offshoot continued straight on toward the border. Buchanan reined up abruptly and spoke to the wondering Juan in a curt voice.

"Fun is fun," he said, "but this is it. *Hasta la vista!*"

"But, amigo —"

"Go on home, Johnny. You've given your folks enough trouble. Me, too."

"I did not intend to make trouble for you, Buchanan."

"Sure, sure. But you know where I'd be if you hadn't pulled that damn-fool shooting last night? Why, man, I'd be at the Whitewater, up in God's country. And with all my goods."

"My father will make up your losses," Juan said.

"I'll make up my own losses, Johnny." He wheeled his mount into the main trail, spurred it to a run without another word or a farewell wave. And he kept the horse at that urgent gait until he knew he was out of earshot. Then he slowed to something more comfortable and cursed the necessity for having to give it to the kid like that.

But what else was there to do. The kid had a bad case of the worships, the same disease Buchanan had had back in West Texas. His hero had been Duke Hazeltine, a wandering wrangler and bronc-buster and the best rifle shot in the world. He'd come into Buchanan's world like a shooting star, made his niche in the boy's memory, then mysteriously departed — followed closely by a U.S. marshal. Buchanan never forgot the list of charges the government man had told his father were outstanding against Duke Hazeltine. He didn't mind the manly things like murder, bank robbery and stage holdup; he could understand how a reckless bravo could fall among bad companions. But he never forgave the swaggering, smiling Duke for forging a bill of sale on a partner's horse. There was something sly and underhanded about that, something that left a bad taste in the mouth.

And so it would be with Juan del Cuervo. He was a young don, the heir to a great ranch. His destiny and Buchanan's were worlds apart, no matter how close Juan thought they were now. Once he rode with Buchanan he would see how different they were, as different as Buchanan was from Duke Hazeltine.

He put the matter out of his mind, considering it settled. The next subject for thought was Lew Agry and a certain purse. He no longer had Pecos for the job, but neither did the sheriff have bully-boy Peek to protect him. Just what help Agry did have in town Buchanan didn't know, but he did have one piece of information Pecos had given him on the ride back from the river.

For a long time after his brother and Carbo had departed for Emerson's, Lew Agry sat motionless behind the desk, feeding bitterly on his rage and frustration. He'd crawled — crawled before them on his belly, and he could see the contempt in Carbo's last glance as though the man were still in the doorway.

Agry raised his right hand level with his eyes and stared at it intently. "My good right arm," Simon used to say in the early days, the pre-Carbo days. "I call the tune," Simon used to say, "and Lew makes them dance."

But the good right arm had a bad tremble in it now, and only by concentrating so hard that sweat beads appeared on his forehead could he make it hold still. He got up then and closed the curtains before the window, retrieved the gunbelt from the wall and buckled it low on his hip. He took a stance with feet wide apart, left arm hanging loose, right arm crooked slightly at the elbow. He inhaled, and expelled the air slowly from his lungs.

"Go!" he shouted, whipping the gun free of the holster and firing at a chest-high crack on the opposite wall. Agry slid the gun back, unloosed the belt and rehung it on the hook.

He'd lost it, lost the touch and the rhythm, the cat sense a gunfighter must have. Just as hazardous, the slug had passed a good four inches to the right of the spot he'd aimed for. The draw was good enough to stop some cowpoke or farmer, but Abe Carbo would have gotten two shots off in less time, dead center.

That, then, was that. All at once he was past caring about what had gone wrong today, about the whereabouts of his missing deputies. *His* missing deputies? He unpinned the star from his rough leather vest and tossed it negligently on the desk. They were on their own. It was every man for himself.

He pulled open the well drawer of the desk, reached down and lifted out a strongbox wrapped in a faded bandanna. On a chain beneath his shirt was the key that opened it. The lid came up to reveal a derringer pocket pistol and a long, intricately designed iron key. He took them out, replaced the box, and from another drawer removed the shoulder holster for the sneak gun. When he was harnessed into that he donned his coat and left the office.

There was sound from the saloon and a faint

light from the hotel, but the street itself was quiet and empty. Lew Agry walked past the hotel and the mercantile until he came to the windowless, new-looking building that was the Agrytown Bank. An enormous padlock hung between the doors and into it Agry inserted the homemade key he carried. The lock sprung and he let himself inside, moving forward unerringly through the blackness. At the big safe he knelt down, struck a light, and from memory of the many times he had observed the operation correctly, dialed the combination. He also knew what he wanted from the safe, and exactly where it was. One was a heavy sack of gold bullion, the other a suitcase crammed with gold certificates. Together they represented the bank's principal assets — some twenty thousand dollars.

He departed from the bank by the rear door, lugged his treasure back along an alleyway and entered the hotel's side door. His own two rooms were a step down the hall and he slipped quietly inside, easing the door shut without a sound. Still moving in the dark, feeling a sense of protection from it, Agry opened a wardrobe trunk and pulled out the empty saddlebags lying in the bottom. These he filled from the sack and the suitcase, distributing the weight evenly, and when the transfer was completed he crossed to the washbowl and pitcher that rested on the small table. He poured the water out slowly, reached into the pitcher with his hand and withdrew Tom Buchanan's purse. This joined the bank's money

— Simon's money for the most part — and the saddlebags were tied closed.

Lew Agry gave a long, satisfied sigh and stood erect. It called for a drink, this did. A drink to Lew Agry, the man with the last laugh. The man who turned defeat into victory, bad luck into good fortune. He went to the bureau, uncorked the bottle and let the whisky splash into the glass. What a good sound that was, he thought. What a happy, prosperous, winning sound. He raised the glass. Here's to you, brother Simon. Here's to you, friend Carbo. He drank it off and hoisted the bottle again. One for the long voyage, he told himself. East, this time. All the way east, then a boat to England. Bad times in Europe now. Twenty-five thousand gold dollars will go a long, long way. Maybe buy me a castle, put a little Frenchie girl in every room. He poured out a third drink.

"Save a little for a thirsty man," said a voice out of that dark silence. The tumbler slipped from Lew Agry's fear-frozen fingers and crashed on the floor.

"Who is it?" he asked hollowly.

"The rannihan, Sheriff. The Mex lover who lives by the gun."

"What do you want?"

"Got any last words?"

"You wouldn't kill me here. You'd never make it out of town."

The cocking of the hammer was a clear, crisp sound.

113

"I'll give you your money, Buchanan!"

"Don't talk about it, Sheriff. Do it."

Agry, as he moved to the saddlebags, was beginning to make out the big figure in the corner.

"What happened?"

"Pecos changed his mind, that's all."

"Is Pecos outside?"

"He's dead."

"Too bad."

"You can tell him when you see him."

Agry made fumbling noises with the thongs that held the bag closed. His body was bent forward with the head held low. Across the room Buchanan could make out only the man's general movements, and his attention was directed to the midsection, where Agry would make a last-ditch draw. Too late he saw that it was a gambler's weapon, a gambler's cross-body draw.

The little gun with the big caliber rocked the room with sound. Three times the Colt gave answer. Then it, like everything else, was quiet.

Chapter Thirteen

ABE Carbo, the man who had seen everything, was hard put to believe what he was seeing now.

He had led the group into Emerson's disordered yard area, and had been the first to dismount. Brushing the querulous old man aside, he had entered the adobe building with a gun in his fist. There stretched on the floor was Waldo Peek, the indestructible man. His jaw hung in a lopsided fashion, his breathing was a groaning, rasping sound, forced through a broken nose and swollen lips. It wasn't even a face, Carbo thought, taken with a morbid fascination for the gargoyle ugliness of it.

In those swift seconds Carbo imagined that an enemy made furious enough had done that to him. He shuddered. Then, blindly, the realization came to him that he had spent a lifetime behind a gun because he so desperately feared a physical beating.

Footsteps sounded at his back and Carbo dragged his eyes away from the wreckage of Waldo Peek.

"So?" Gomez said tensely. "Where is the boy?"

"Maybe he knows," Carbo said, indicating the worried Hamp Horne who stood in the corner.

"They took the Mex with 'em," Hamp said.

"They? Who?" Carbo snapped.

"Pecos," he said. "Pecos and the hardcase. The big guy."

"Buchanan?"

"Yeah. But Pecos got killed up the road. Waldo got him."

Gomez stepped past Abe Carbo, throwing caution to the wind in his sudden excitement.

"Buchanan?" he asked, echoing Carbo's disbelief. "He is with Juan del Cuervo?"

Simon Agry pounded in. "Good God! Is that Waldo Peek?"

"What the hardcase left of him," Hamp Horne said. "Me and the old man drug him inside. Ivy got hisself killed at the start of it. He's outside somewheres."

Gomez was no longer interested. He had swung around, started for the door.

"Where you going, amigo?" Abe Carbo asked and the segundo's face broke into a broad grin. He looked like a happy bulldog.

"Home, amigo," Gomez said. "I'm going home."

"He's got the paper you want," Carbo said to Simon Agry.

"Hand it over," Simon said, bolstered by the gun in Carbo's grasp. "I kept my part of the deal."

Gomez laughed in his face.

"Let's have it!" Simon demanded.

"Or what, señor?" Gomez nodded his head toward the doorway. "Carbo cannot shoot in all directions at once. In the crossfire your body will

116

be an inviting target."

"Don't let him bluff you, Si," Carbo said goadingly, richly enjoying the play of emotions on Agry's mobile face. But Simon was mindful only of Gomez's threat and the fact that he was the most exposed man in the room.

"The hell with a scrap of paper," he blustered. "A deal's a deal, and by Judas I mean to collect!"

Gomez laughed again, then held his fist toward Abe Carbo, the thumb pointed upward.

"Until then, señores," he said and walked out on them. The men inside could hear his voice shouting the news, hear the vaqueros send up a joyous whoop as they wheeled their blooded mounts and sped away.

Buchanan! Gomez thought emotionally. Was there ever such a one for being in the right place at the right time? Never! Viva Buchanan, the patron saint of Rancho del Rey!

"Which trail do we take, Café?" Ramon asked when the juncture was approaching.

"Through Agrytown! I would stop long enough to spit at the ground before the sheriff!"

"I have never seen you in such spirits, *viejo.*"

"Tonight in my quarters," Gomez promised, "we will drink until the vat is dry."

Ramon blinked. Was this Gomez, the man of stone?

Not even the prospect of hanging had saddened Juan's heart quite so deeply as Buchanan's forsaking him on the trail. Perhaps it was the abruptness of it, the fact that at the very moment Buchanan announced it Juan's thoughts had been overflowing with the happy incident of bringing his great friend to the hacienda.

It had been a hard and stunning blow, and Juan found himself almost incapable of sensation, of movement, as Buchanan's horse pounded away into the night and Buchanan's harsh words echoed and re-echoed in his ears. Then, letting the animal set whatever pace it desired, Juan no longer cared where he went.

But a mile later he suddenly reined up. Had it been Buchanan's decision to make? Because the man did not choose to ride with him, was that any reason Juan must ride where Buchanan commanded? No, came the defiant answer, and with that as justification he swung back to find the trail to Agrytown

Then another argument stiffened his resolve. Why, he asked himself, was Buchanan making this side trip? Answer: To retrieve his purse from the sheriff. And hadn't the purse been stolen on Juan's account? Therefore, to aid Buchanan was only simple courtesy — unrelated to friendship, loyalty or any such sentimentality — and only what would be expected of a Del Cuervo. He spurred his mount forward.

When he came to the town, however, he made his way cautiously. It would not do to undo everything that had been accomplished and fall into the sheriff's hands again. In addition to the unpleasantness of being hanged, such a fiasco would only convince Buchanan of his unreliability, or whatever it was that Buchanan objected to about him.

So he moved along warily, keeping to the shadows, and finally dismounted altogether, hitching his horse to a post and proceeding on foot. His destination was the sheriff's office, which he imagined to be Buchanan's destination as well, and when he passed the saloon his mind was flooded with the remembered violence inside the place and right here on the sidewalk. And only twenty-four hours ago. It seemed as if an eternity had transpired since he'd ridden here to kill Roy Agry . . .

Juan ducked quickly into an alleyway the instant he saw the sheriff's office door opened and Lew Agry step into the street. He watched as Agry peered carefully up and down, then moved resolutely along the row of buildings. Where was Buchanan? Was he, too, observing the man from concealment?

Now what? The bank! The sheriff was entering the bank, in the dead of the night, and his very furtiveness gave away his guilt. *Ai, caramba,* what a family of thieves and villains! But where was Buchanan?

Agry was inside the bank now and Juan could only wait to see what would develop. Five minutes later he was still waiting. Ten minutes passed.

At the sound of the shots he froze. Two men put their heads out of the saloon, glanced around the quiet street, and then returned to their drinking. But though the silence had satisfied them, it only worried the boy. He placed the source of the firing at the hotel, and when he saw the clerk come out onto the porch obviously looking for help, he knew that whatever the trouble was it had occurred there.

Well, this was what he had come for, he reminded himself. This was the obligation he must discharge. Juan crossed the street at a lope, decided against a direct entry into the hotel, and went up the alley that stretched alongside. He found the door Lew Agry had used — and all but stumbled over the crawling figure of Tom Buchanan.

"Amigo. You are hit!"

"Is that Johnny?"

"*Sí*. Can you walk if I raise you, Buchanan?"

"I told you to go home."

"Can you walk?"

"Don't know. Slug got me in the shoulder," he said wonderingly. "Don't know why it caved in the damn legs."

"Try to stand," Juan said, helping the big man aloft with an effort.

"Must be built backwards —"

Juan got him out into the alley, had him started toward the street when that exit was abruptly blocked by a group of excited men.

"Hold it where you are!" Amos Agry shouted to them.

"Other way, Johnny. *Vamos!*"

"I said hold it!" A shot came winging after them.

"Man," Buchanan said feelingly, "some people just can't mind their own business." He reached around the boy's body, slipped the .45 from its holster and sent back a wildly effective fusillade that scattered their tormentors and gave them the temporary protection of the bank building.

"Let me down, kid."

"No." Juan resisted Buchanan's efforts to remove his supporting shoulder.

"Use your head. We both can't make it and I got what I came for."

"Is the sheriff dead?"

"Surprised if he wasn't. Now let go of me."

They could hear stealthy footsteps in the alleyway, and shouts on the street beyond directing an encirclement of the area.

"Get out of here, Johnny."

"Look, Buchanan — the rear of the bank is open!" He got the other man moving toward the door, pulled him inside and locked it closed.

"Now you've fixed yourself," Buchanan said angrily. "How you going to bust out of here?"

"You'll think of something, amigo."

"Yeah. Me and Duke Hazeltine."

"What did you say?"

"I said you're just another damn loco Mex." There was a heavy thrusting at the door. "Load this shooter," Buchanan said, handing Juan the emptied Colt. "Then see if you can find the teller's cage. There ought to be some weapons handy there."

As Juan disengaged himself, Buchanan leaned an arm against the wall to hold himself upright. The temporary paralysis that had seized the entire left side of his body was retreating, leaving him steadier on his legs but paining like hell in the shoulder region.

The pounding and the yelling increased in tempo outside. Something heavy, an iron post or a log, had been brought to bear against the door.

"I found another gun,"' Juan said, returning to his side.

"How do you feel?"

"Very good. Very scared, too."

"Yeah. Now when that door gives, aim low and shoot fast. We don't have a chance, but let's raise as much hell as we can."

With that the door did give. The two trapped men threw a withering blast into the opening, felling one of their attackers, who gave an anguished scream, and driving the others back. But even as Buchanan and Juan reloaded, the doors behind them swung open and a second force swarmed inside.

"Low and fast, kid," Buchanan shouted. "Deal 'em hell till the deck's gone!"

Gomez's mind was so full of Buchanan that when the sound of the firing came to him the association was immediate. Who else could stir the hornet's nest of Agrytown to such a fury? *"Andamos!"* he roared, roweling his horse, flattening his body over its neck in the way of vaqueros and literally flying over the ground. Ramon and the other two men, catching fire from their leader, made a race of it, and they came down Agrytown's main street four abreast.

Those townspeople who had just discovered the bank's front door unexplainedly open poured inside with uneasy minds. Only Mexicans rode with that particular rhythm, and by now they knew that one of the two trapped in there was the Mexican kid. They didn't like the situation any more, and the quicker-witted among them reversed direction and ran for cover.

"Low and fast, kid," Buchanan shouted. "Wheel and deal!" He fired at one door and then another, seeing the consternation among their enemies at the front of the building but not understanding it. Then there was a great racket of shooting from the street and all the opposition up there collapsed.

"What is happening?" Juan asked.

"I think it's your Uncle Coffee," Buchanan said happily. "Let's have a looksee." He sent a steady stream of fire into the rear door, covering their back-stepping progress to the front of the building. The war in the street, meanwhile, had fallen off to nothing.

"Buchanan?" came Gomez's anxious voice. "Is it you?"

"And a friend," Juan called back. "Is it clear out there?"

"Safe as a cathedral, señor. The rats have scurried back to their holes."

The two men stepped to the street.

"Where are your mounts?"

Juan pointed to where he'd parked his down the street, and a vaquero peeled off to get it.

"Where's yours, Buchanan?" Juan asked, but the big man was leaning his weight against the building, strangely silent. With the stimulus of the battle gone he had been overcome with this irresistible desire to sleep forever. Even as Juan and Gomez approached him his head fell forward on his chest and he sank slowly to the ground.

Chapter Fourteen

AMOS AGRY had been the first to discover his cousin Lew's death, the first to sound the alarm and the first to quit when the going got hot. But he had a little more incentive than saving his skin. All through the action, in fact, his thoughts had kept wandering back to the scene in Lew's room.

The big one had been just barely stirring when Amos went in there and glimpsed the damage by candlelight. Buchanan's fingers gripped the leather purse Amos remembered from the night before, but what really took the clerk's attention was the cascade of big-denomination certificates that littered the floor beneath the open saddle-bag and lay across the arm and chest of the lifeless sheriff. Buchanan had moved then, and Amos fled to get help.

Now he was back in the room, working feverishly, expecting Cousin Simon to arrive hard on the heels of the Mexicans. He stuffed the spilled money back inside the bag, fumbled clumsily with the thongs, finally fastened them and then dragged the heavy burden to the door. He paused there, trembling, sweating clammily from fear and expectation. He opened the door and peered down the hallway. No one should be there, and no one was. The only guest during the past month had been Buchanan. The only persons using the place were himself and Cousin Lew.

Cousin Lew. Amos couldn't resist the impulse to look back over his shoulder at the grotesquely fallen figure of the man who had ridden so rough-shod over him all their lives. See the swaggering bully-boy now. How many times did he call me stupid? Amos asked himself. Who was stupid now — dead, with his sneering mouth agape, his sardonic eyes wide and staring?

"I hope you burn in hell, Lew," Amos said aloud. "I hope you catch it good."

He bent down, and with a great effort shouldered the saddlebags and carried them down the hallway. Suddenly he stopped and his knees almost caved in beneath him. Horses! Simon and Carbo were here. All right, stay calm. Take the money out onto the front porch, tell Simon a story about how you had saved it for him.

But wasn't there still time? Wasn't this the big chance, the last chance to be everything but a lackey all his life? Simon wouldn't thank him for rescuing the money; there'd be no reward. All he'd get would be more orders, more dull and dirty jobs to do. His father, the uncle of Simon and Lew, had taken a hand in raising them when their own father had gone to prison. He'd taken the whip to them, as he had to his own children, and it seemed to Amos that his cousins still resented those hidings and were taking it out on him.

Instead of taking the money out to the porch,

Amos turned and began climbing the service stairway to the floor above. He halted at the top for a breath, then continued down the corridor until he came to the ladder that led to the attic. He dragged the saddlebags behind him, slid the trap door aside and got the heavy weights up the ladder and onto the attic floor. He didn't even bother to climb in there and conceal them, but replaced the door and came back down. Amos had just reached the first floor again when the front door of the hotel burst open and Simon charged through the lobby.

"Where's my brother?" Simon shouted wildly.

Amos pointed to Lew's room, followed the other man at a respectful distance. Simon stopped in the doorway and stared at the body with an incredulous expression, then went in and stood looking down at it in fascination. After a moment his head came up and his eyes were snapping.

"Who killed him? Who's got the money from the bank?"

"Buchanan," Amos told him. "I tried to hole him up in there but he got help from the Mex riders."

Simon left the room in a rage, went looking for Abe Carbo and found him talking with a group before the open bank building. He motioned to the gunman imperiously, and his anger mounted at the time it took Carbo to break off his conference and saunter toward him.

"Damn it, come when you're called!" Simon growled, but Carbo didn't seem to hear. He was, in fact, deep in speculation. Finding that safe broken into had dealt Abe Carbo a rather nasty shock, which would have surprised Simon Agry had he known. Carbo's bandit heritage had led him to take a proprietary interest in those thousands of dollars, and now he felt a very personal loss.

"Get a war party together," Agry said. "We're riding!"

"Riding where?"

"To Del Cuervo's. Buchanan and Gomez stole my money."

That didn't jibe with the answers Carbo had just gotten from the eyewitnesses. They told him that Buchanan had been lifted onto Gomez's horse, and there was no mention of any heavy money sacks. Besides, the padlock had not been shot away but opened with a key.

"Lew's got it," Carbo said, repeating his first thought about the theft.

"Lew's in his room. Dead."

Carbo brushed past the fat man and hurried into the hotel. He picked up a lamp from the desk and made his way to the rear room. He turned the body roughly over, then pulled it out of the way while he stooped down to peer beneath the bed. He reached in and pulled out the empty sack and suitcase.

"That's them!" Simon said excitedly from behind him. "By God, it *was* Lew. And the hardcase killed him and took it away."

"Could be," Carbo said, thinking that might have been the way of it. The witnesses had ob-

128

viously watched from cover. They could have missed the transfer of the money. He reasoned, too, that besides himself only Buchanan had the excuse and the nerve to brace Lew Agry.

"Then what the hell are we waiting for?" Simon demanded impatiently.

Carbo shook his head. "You don't have the warriors for the job," he said.

"We beat them last time —"

"As I remember, Lew had a hand in that. Lew, Pecos, Lafe, and Waldo Peek. We got to replace those guns, Si."

"By hell, Abe, you're the last man I ever expected to show a yellow streak."

Carbo regarded Simon Agry thoughtfully. Why not puncture this bag of wind right now and be done with it? he asked himself.

"I spoke hasty," Agry said into the silence, almost as though he read Carbo's mind. "This is no time for us to fall out."

"You're right, Si."

"What plans you got for getting back that gold?"

"Like I said, we got to hire some gunhands."

"Where?"

"I'll mosey north aways. Be back in a week."

"A *week?* Buchanan'll be out of the country —"

"I don't think so. Don Pedro is going to want to show his gratitude. And you know how long that takes a Mexican."

CHAPTER FIFTEEN

HE is a huge one," the Indian girl reported to Maria del Cuervo in the morning. "Just as Amaya described."

"When did he arrive?"

"In the dead of the night. Along with Señor Juan —"

"Juan?"

"Oh, señorita, the stories that are flying! Your brother killed the man who attacked you —"

Maria gasped.

"— and was himself captured and condemned to the gallows!"

"No!"

"And Don Pedro sent Gomez to ransom him. But the big one rescued him. Just as —"

"It seems that *he* found you, señorita. Not Gomez."

"Oh!"

"But you were unconscious," Felice said loyally to the blushing girl.

"But how was I dressed?"

"God knows," Felice said.

"And him. How is he called?"

"Buchanan," the Indian said, giggling. "What a funny name."

"Their names are all very strange," Maria said. "What does he look like?"

"Ferocious, so Tia Rosa says. And all covered with blood."

Maria jumped up from the bed. "Blood?" she cried. "Blood!"

"A bullet wound. Tia Rosa cut the bullet out of his body."

"But he will surely die."

"That would be better, I think," Felice said.

"I must see him first," Maria said, putting a robe over her cotton nightgown.

"Señorita! What are you thinking?"

"He is in my brother's rooms?"

"But you cannot go there. You are not dressed."

"There may not be time. It is my duty."

Maria slipped from the room, and her maid guessed that it was more female curiosity than duty that called her. Doña Isabel, she also guessed, would be scandalized. It was not the custom in this particular hacienda for an unmarried daughter to go calling on guests in their bedrooms.

"*Venite*," Juan said in answer to the soft rapping on the door. "Come in." The door opened, and at sight of his sister's wide-eyed face peering around he laughed in pure joy.

"Maria!"

"Oh, Juan! I have heard such a tale about you!" She came in, her glance darting in every direction, and when there was no sign of the stranger man she went forward to embrace her brother warmly.

"And what have you heard?"

"The most terrible things. That you killed Roy

— that you killed a man. That you were going to be hanged . . ."

"You are avenged, little sister, and all is well. But you had better leave before my friend Buchanan wanders in from the other room. He is, of necessity, without clothing."

"But he is dying, isn't he?"

"El Hombre? *Por Dios,* no! He is beyond destruction."

"But the blood?"

"Blood? Buchanan bleeds as I sweat. If I could show you the floor of our cell in the jail —"

"*Madre mia!* You went to jail with him?"

"He went with me, sister. He sought to free me from the deputy and was himself terribly beaten. *Ai,* but he repaid them both for that indignity."

"What — what did he do?"

"When you are married to Sebastian Diaz I will describe the whole adventure. It is not for your tender ears now."

"What did Buchanan say of me?" Maria asked, unable to stifle the question.

"Of you? Nothing. Oh, yes! He inquired after your health."

"He said nothing of finding me?"

"*Nada.*"

"Nothing of how I was — how I looked?"

"*Nada,*" Juan said a little impatiently. "Buchanan wastes few words on what is unimportant."

"Unimportant?"

"Of course. To El Hombre you are the little girl, as you are to me. Now the little girl had better go. If my friend saw you he would gobble you in one bite."

Maria stood straighter, indignantly, and it would have been apparent to anyone but an older brother that there was something more substantial than a little girl within the robe.

The door opened behind them and Gomez looked in.

"The don would like to see us in his study," the segundo announced, and from the look in his eyes he had made good to Ramon about the party in his quarters.

"Tío Café, you are ill!" Maria told him anxiously.

"It will pass, señorita. If God is willing."

Juan laughed. "Tío Café does penance, Maria," he told her. "He sins rarely, but then it is a great one."

This was man talk, and though Maria understood that Gomez was suffering from too much wine it was fashionable to pretend she knew nothing of such things. Juan put his arm around Café's shoulder then and they left, forgetting her altogether.

The door closed, and the silence was so intimate that it appalled her senses. This, very definitely, was a transgression of the strict code that governed her behavior. To visit a dying man was permissible. To be alone in a room with a brother was allowed. But not this — especially since she had

133

been warned that the stranger might be up and about.

Maria felt properly heady and maidenly as she tiptoed to the connecting door and very, very timidly turned the handle in her trembling fingers. She opened the door the merest crack and put her eye to it, almost afraid of what she would see in there. But all she saw was the back of a man's shaggy head, the tremendous outline of a giant beneath the blanket.

Buchanan stirred and Maria all but shrieked. He turned over on his back and the blanket fell away to reveal the bandage Tia Rosa had fashioned over his left shoulder. The girl raised her eyes to the man's face, and quite unconsciously she pulled the door wide and stepped through, moving closer to the bed as though pulled by invisible strings.

Ferocious. Felice's word came back to her as she stared down at that powerful, angular face with its broken nose, its scars and the wild growth of black beard. A shiver passed through her body as she thought of such a rough one coming upon her helpless and naked in the brush. But the very thought begged its own question: If he was such a fierce type then why had he delivered her to safety? For the first time, Maria was realizing that it was not something she had dreamed. It had been this man's hands pressing beneath her ribs, forcing the water out of her lungs, making her breathe. And it was no dream being wrapped in that warm blanket and lifted like a feather.

After that she remembered nothing but the vague sound of Juan's voice in the darkness. . . .

Maria found herself gazing directly into Buchanan's inquisitive blue eyes.

"How are you?" he asked.

Maria opened her lips but no sound came forth. It seemed to the girl that she was poised on tiptoe, that she was about to plunge headlong into those bottomless azure depths. Then he was smiling at her, smiling with nothing held in reserve, and it showed her the full lips, the generous, good-humored mouth that had been hidden by the heavy beard.

"I am fine, thank you," she said mechanically. "And you?"

"Hard to say. This your bunk?"

"It is Juan's bed."

"Feels awful soft," Buchanan said. "Thought it was yours, seeing you dressed for bed, and all."

Maria raised her hand to her throat, closing the top of the wrapper. "I am not dressed for bed," she said. "I consider myself fully clothed."

"So do I. Where is Johnny, anyhow?"

"John-ny?"

"The kid," Buchanan said. "Your brother."

"You are such an old man then?"

"Going on thirty-one," he said.

"I will be nineteen years old in July," Maria said. "That is only twelve years younger."

Buchanan laughed. "A lifetime," he said.

"My father is older than my mother by fifteen

135

years. There is not a lifetime separating them."

"Glad to hear it. But where's Johnny?"

"He and Gomez are with my father. Is there something you need?"

"My duds," Buchanan said. "You wouldn't believe this, but you're talking to a man that's naked as a jaybird."

"You have the protection of the blanket," Maria said, shocked at her own audacity. "That is more than I had when you found me."

"Well, that's true enough."

"Oh! How could you?"

"How could I what?"

"Admit such a thing! That you saw me — nude!"

"Why, I didn't give it a thought, honey."

"You didn't?"

Buchanan's expression showed that he was completely at sea with this girl. Nothing he could think of to say could please her.

"You were just a half-drowned little rat when I found you," he said good-naturedly, appeasingly. "Damn fine figure of a woman, but I just plainly didn't pay much attention —"

He thought for a moment she was going to strike him. Instead she whirled around and swept out of the room. And just as well, for within the next minute the door opened again and there was a delegation come to visit him.

"My parents could not wait to meet you," Juan said, bringing Don Pedro and Doña Isabel inside. He made the introductions very formally and Buchanan acknowledged them with as much dignity as he could summon. Traveling with Campos as he had, Buchanan's experience with the pure-blooded aristocracy of Mexico was nonexistent, and now he regarded these two with frank curiosity.

"Señor," Don Pedro said very simply, "how can I ever repay you?" Gomez and his wife glanced at him in surprise. Not only had he begun his first conversation with Buchanan using the familiar te, but there had been marked emotion in his voice.

"Your boy saved my bacon last night," Buchanan answered just as directly. "I guess that puts the score all even." He turned to Doña Isabel. "You've got a fine family, ma'am."

"*Gracias.* I'm sure your people must be proud of their fine son."

Buchanan didn't know about that, but her words had a good sound to them. They made him feel as though he almost belonged to someone instead of the footloose ramstam that he knew himself to be.

"How is your wound?" Don Pedro asked solicitously.

"A little stiff this morning," Buchanan answered. "But I'll be able to ride."

"Ride?"

Buchanan grinned wryly. "I passed through this neck of the woods two days ago," he said. "I'm kind of anxious to make a little better progress."

"You have some urgent business in the north?"

"Not that I know of, Don Pedro, and I hope you and the lady don't take this personal. But I'm grown a little sour on Mexico and some of the people I've had dealings with."

"The land is not at rest, señor. I apologize for anything that my countrymen have done to you."

Buchanan waved his big arm magnanimously. "Don't give it a second thought," he said. "Fact is, I'm a little more fed up with some of my own fellow citizens. The Agrytown breed, anyway."

"Yes," Don Pedro said. "I would certainly not want to judge all Americans by the acts of the Agrys."

"Fair enough. And I won't measure out Mexicans by that — by Campos."

Don Pedro smiled. "To celebrate this treaty between our two nations, then, will you stay and accept the hospitality of my house?"

"A *gran fiesta*, Buchanan!" Juan said eagerly.

"Well, sure! I guess I could stand a little partyin'. Thanks very much."

"The thanks are ours," Don Pedro said, and he and his family left. Then, as Doña Isabel had instructed previously, servant girls arrived and began filling the tub with buckets of steaming hot water. Buchanan followed the movements of one of the girls with interest. She was a head taller than the others, slimmer, and with hair that was not the universal black but the color of burnished copper.

Nor was she unaware of his glance, undulating her supple hips as she worked, and leaning far over the tub to give him a delightful view of her breasts from the bed.

Nor was Gomez missing any of the flirtation. He wondered, in fact, if it might not be the means of prolonging Buchanan's stay.

"Lilita," Gomez said. "Make a proper greeting to the great benefactor of your *patrón* and mistress."

The girl curtsied gracefully, seemingly unmindful of the fit of giggling that suddenly took her companions.

"We are in your debt, señor."

"Glad to hear it. Tell me, have you ever been to San Javier?"

"I was born in San Javier."

"Nice little town."

"If one likes bandits, fighting and murder," Lilita said. "I prefer it here."

Gomez gave her backside a whack. "What do you know of bandits? You were not eight years old when you came to this house."

Lilita rubbed where it stung. "I know more than you think, Tio Café! About a lot of things."

He laughed. "About men?"

"Pouf! What is there to know about men?"

"If you are so worldly-wise then, perhaps you will stay and bathe our guest?"

Lilita swung around to Buchanan and gazed full in his face.

"I am only a servant," she said quietly. "What

the guest of Don Pedro orders me to do, I will do."

Buchanan met her eyes levelly. An impish grin spread across his face.

"Gomez," he said, "I guess you don't know these girls from San Javier. She's liable to scrape the skin off my back."

"That is the risk you take," Lilita told him.

"Then go, little wildcat," Gomez said. "Perhaps if you are lucky the señor will dance one dance with you tonight."

"And if he is lucky I will have one to spare." She left with a toss of her long hair and an impudent swing of her hips, and the other girls scampered out in her wake.

Within minutes, Maria del Cuervo was getting a full report.

"She was without shame," Felice said breathlessly. "And to think that my own brother Amaya pays court to such a vixen."

"He and every unmarried vaquero here," Maria said. "She has a very beautiful figure."

"Too skinny," said the plumpish little Indian. "What would a man want with such a scarecrow?"

"You, yourself, said that Buchanan stared at her openly."

"I am talking of Mexican men, señorita. Who pays attention to *Americanos?*"

"I am surprised at Gomez," Maria said. "As majordomo he should preserve his dignity."

"Something has happened to him," Felice said.

"This Buchanan is a bad influence. Imagine telling her to bathe a man. An unmarried girl!"

"But you say she would have done it?"

"I am positive. Then the señor made some other reference to San Javier and it was over."

"What is so special about San Javier?"

"I have never been there," Felice said self-righteously. "But it must be a scandalous place."

"Yes," Maria said, a little wistfully. "And Buchanan is a scandalous hombre."

Chapter Sixteen

ABE CARBO had no intention of going "north aways" or of waiting a week. He was going after the money himself, and the best way he knew — alone. With a gambler's audaciousness he packed his provisions with Simon Agry looking on, took a thousand dollars from the man as advance payment to the imaginary gun fighters he would hire, and rode out. On the outskirts of town he glanced back without regret for what he was leaving. Without the money from the bank, control of Agrytown held no particular interest.

At the intersection he doubled back toward the border, unworried about being followed. Even if Simon didn't trust him, it was something that Simon couldn't dare admit. For Agry had maneuvered himself into a position where he had to depend on Carbo or go down. No money, no protection, no friends. Poor Simon.

Carbo laughed aloud and put him out of his mind completely. What he did think about was the job at hand. He guessed that the owner of Rancho del Rey would be in a holiday mood, and that the safe return of his son without having to pay the ransom would call for a fiesta comparable to a christening or a wedding.

Nor would they be too much concerned about a quick reprisal from Agry. Gomez knew the manpower situation as well as Carbo did. Agry simply didn't have the guns for a frontal attack, and anything short of a U.S. cavalry troop would be cut to ribbons. A vaquero was loyal first and last to his home ranch, and in defense of it one was worth any six raiders. That was why they made such poor soldiers. Fighting for anything so impersonal as a federal government failed to arouse them to the necessary pitch.

But Gomez would not expect one man to attack — would not because he had no idea how jealously Abe Carbo regarded those sacks of gold. They were the big strike from which the gambler meant to launch his fortune. And Carbo also meant to use the fiesta in his own favor. Some would drink until they passed out, others would either dance themselves into exhaustion or go off into some secluded brush with a jug and a woman. Carbo knew what fiestas were like and what one sober man could get away with.

He crossed over the border and came onto Del Cuervo land just as the sun was sinking. He made his first stop at a line camp, unconcernedly built a fire in the shack, ate his supper and lay down to nap. It would be many hours before the fiesta was at the stage Abe Carbo wanted it to be.

Three times Amos Agry had slipped away to the attic, staying only long enough to count a small portion of the money and hide it among the beams and beneath floorboards. And each time he had come back to the desk with the same

143

nagging problem: What was he going to do with it? How was he going to get it safely out of town? His plans for the gold were neither as rapacious as his cousin Lew's had been, nor as ambitious as Carbo's. Amos saw himself returning to Kentucky in style, of buying into a hotel, perhaps raising some thoroughbreds to race on Sunday afternoons in Lexington. He could feel the silk dress shirt he would wear in the evenings, the tweed suit imported from Scotland. Amos's palms fairly itched to start spending his hoard.

He had heard Simon's conversation with Carbo last night and he'd seen the gunman ride off today in search of fighters. Suppose they did capture Buchanan but didn't find the money? Buchanan would say that he left the saddlebags in the room with Lew. Then Simon would realize that there was only one man who'd had both the time and the opportunity to take them out of there. And Amos didn't doubt for an instant that his cousin would hang him to the nearest tree.

A neat problem, but not without its even neater solution. If, for instance, Buchanan had warning that Simon and Carbo were coming after him; if he were told that they meant to kill him on sight as repayment for Lew's death — then Buchanan would either leave the country or ambush Simon and kill him. Amos would have the freedom of the money and all the leisure he needed to get back to Kentucky.

At sundown he saddled a horse and rode for Rancho del Rey.

On four different occasions that day four different vaqueros had found some urgent business that called them to the hacienda. And while there each had found time to search out Lilita and upbraid her for her actions in the *Americano's* bedroom. To each the girl replied that none of them was married to her yet and whatever she did — if she did anything — was not his concern.

The consensus was that she had bathed Buchanan, and, busily soaping and scrubbing her own body that evening, Lilita told herself angrily, she rather wished that she had. Why not? It was quite clear to the girl, after an entire day spent examining her thoughts on the matter, that she was very seriously in love with Buchanan.

She had suspected that her feelings were a great deal more than coquettish during that almost frightening moment when he had looked deep into her heart and discovered her secret. And what secret would a lowly servant girl from San Javier harbor? Simply that she recognized no man's privilege to order her to do anything. For that heresy men would whip her with the lash, drag her naked through the streets, call down God's vengeance and make her do penance for the rest of her life. The men of Rancho del Rey would. But Buchanan had accepted it without question. For that she loved him, and womanlike, would do anything he ordered her to.

She had also been guided by the prediction. Two years before, when Lilita was sixteen, Juanita the gypsy woman had passed through and read her palm. The wise old gypsy, taking note of the lithe, developing young body, the fluid, amorous eyes, had been on safe ground when she predicted that the girl's life among the stolid, hardworking people of Rancho del Rey would be a stormy one. Only a strong man, a big man with the same adventurous spirit, would be able to keep her content. The gypsy had set the date of his arrival two years ahead, knowing full well that things would have to reach a climax by that time.

So to walk in there and find Buchanan, with his easy acceptance of her rebellious ideas, his tremendous physical attraction, his appreciation of San Javier — all that was too much for such a girl of passion to resist. The thing now was to get him in the same frame of mind, and to that end she opened the bottle of perfume the gypsy had given her and dressed with great care.

And in another part of the house Maria del Cuervo dressed with Buchanan in mind. Her brief conversation with him this morning had thrown her badly off balance, made her question the very fundamentals of her moral convictions. Was modesty in a woman a virtue or an affectation? Should she feel mortally embarrassed in Buchanan's presence, or treat the incident as carelessly as he did? He had made her feel like a foolish child, and what struck at her pride was that he obviously hadn't intended to.

Felice came in with the newly pressed gown that Maria had chosen. She had worn it once before, as a bridesmaid at her cousin Julia's wedding one year ago, and though it was the most decorous costume in her wardrobe — high-necked and long-sleeved — the twelve months that the girl had spent maturing gave the dress some very prominent and eye-catching curves that the dressmaker had never intended.

"I think maybe the doña should inspect you," Felice said nervously.

"Nonsense. I am practically a married woman."

"I wish you were officially one, señorita. In this gown you are likely to give drinking men ideas that are not so good for them."

"The more you say, Felicita, the more you encourage me. Perhaps I shall have all my clothes taken in here and there."

"Señorita — you are going to marry the young Señor Diaz?"

"Of course."

"You love him very much?"

"Of course."

"And this Buchanan? You feel nothing for him?"

"Don't be absurd!" Maria laughed. "What could I feel for anyone so gauche as that?"

Despite her young mistress's assurances, Felice found time soon after that to have a private audience with Doña Isabel. And Isabel, whose Castilian blood fairly oozed romantic intrigue, considered the Indian girl's report and went

147

straight to the room where Buchanan was staying.

Buchanan had trouble enough. An hour before
he had been visited by a gaunt, hollow-eyed old
man carrying lathered soap, a rusted straight razor
and bandages. He introduced himself as Silvio,
said that Gomez had sent him and ordered Buchanan to lie down on the bed and not move.
Especially not move.

Thus the shaving operation had begun, the first
for Buchanan since the big run-in with Campos
— how long ago? Ten days? Two weeks? And
though the skin of his face had healed over some
and was not so blood-raw, Silvio's dull, nicked
blade not only opened the old wounds but dug
fresh pieces out of him.

"*Por favor* — do not move!"

"Man, I got a pocketknife would shave me
smoother than that thing."

"Please. No talking, no moving."

"You ought to open up a store next to the
undertaker," Buchanan growled at him, and
the old man found that a funny remark. "I *am*
the undertaker," he said. "*Por favor*, lie still."

That ordeal ended, the old man proceeded to
cut off handfuls of Buchanan's hair, comb out
the loose ends and cut again. All this, with his
customer prone and without consultation. When
Buchanan was permitted to stand, feeling
strangely like a man emerging from his own coffin,
he was handed a mirror.

"Good Godamighty! What've you been doing to me, anyhow?"

"Merely a shave and a haircut," Silvio answered.

"You got me all Spanished up, hombre. What am I doing with these sideburns and chin whiskers?"

"The goatee, señor, is most fashionable."

"Not in West Texas. Hand over those clippers." Buchanan snipped away the rather distinguished-looking little beard, then cut the sideburns from his cheeks until the hair was level with the lobes of his ears. Silvio looked on in somber disapproval, picked up his tools and left.

Gomez himself came in next, carrying an armload of clothing.

"So that is what you look like, *amigo mio.*"

"Take it or leave it, ramrod. What's all that fancy stuff?"

"What you will wear at the fiesta."

"Hell, I'll put on my regular duds."

"Impossible. They were burned last night."

"Burned?"

"By my orders. *Caramba,* even the dogs put their tails between their legs and slinked away when they scented you last night."

"Then they're afraid of good honest sweat. I laid out forty gold dollars for that outfit in Sonora."

"Two years ago, perhaps. The boots I kept out and had polished. The cobbler says it is their baptism."

"Campos," Buchanan said, "didn't run any spit-and-polish outfit."

"You sound bitter, amigo, whenever you mention the famous liberator of Mexico."

"Bitter? Not me, old partner. I shook the bastard's hand and came away with all five fingers intact. Me and Campos are like brothers."

Gomez enjoyed this natural man and his laughter came full and unbridled. "Get yourself dressed, Buchanan. There is nothing so ridiculous as an angry man who is also naked."

Scowling, the big man put his legs through the one-piece, knee-length linen underwear, shrugged into the white, ruffled silk shirtwaist which Gomez tied behind him. The deep-napped, luxuriant felt trousers came next, trousers that hung loose at the calf but hugged his thighs and hips snugly.

"Where'd these come from?" Buchanan asked.

"Believe it or not, Don Pedro had them cut from cloth by the tailor this morning and made in one day. A miracle, if you knew José the tailor."

"I just wish he knew me a little better. Man, this outfit is close."

"The fashion, Buchanan. Now let's try the vest."

It was a sleeved vest, of the same black cloth but trimmed lavishly with interlaced silver cloth. And for all the outsize allowances that José had been admonished to make, the jacket still fit snugly across the shoulders. Buchanan sat down on the edge of the bed and pulled on his gleaming black boots. He stood up.

"Amigo," Gomez said, "you are a thing of rare beauty. Come view yourself in the mirror."

Buchanan looked, and a self-conscious smile lit his face.

"God damn," he said. "If Campos could only see me now."

"Wait till Lilita sees you."

Buchanan caught Gomez's eyes in the mirror.

"Don't go pushing nothing with that one," he said. "That little girl's no fly-by-night."

"You, too?" Gomez asked, laughing. "She has my vaqueros swimming in the head. They rant in their sleep about her."

"All I'm saying is don't push. Let nature take its course."

"You are frightened of her! You — *El Hombre!*"

"She's no fly-by-night," Buchanan repeated.

"*Por Dios,* I think you are being serious."

Buchanan turned around, put his hands on Gomez's shoulders. "Don't push it," he said. "I'm riding out of here in the morning. I don't want to take her with me."

"*Por que?* Why do you ride away? If the girl pleases you why not stay here with her — with us? I know that Don Pedro wants to give you the north section at the border. We would ranch it all together, you, Juan and myself. Three good comrades."

"Man, you're putting pearls before swine. I'm Tom Buchanan, the saddlebum."

"No! You are a rancher, *hijo.* A cattleman if I ever saw one."

"Damn it, Gomez, stop putting big ideas into an empty head!"

The door opened and Doña Isabel stood in the entrance. "What big ideas are those, Señor Tomaso?" she asked.

"I guess I did raise my voice, ma'am. Sorry."

"No," the lady said. "It is your indulgence I beg, for listening so long outside your door. I should have come in immediately you mentioned my servant, Lilita." She smiled at both men. "I'm afraid I found the conversation too exciting to interrupt. The maid takes your fancy, señor?"

"She's awful pretty," Buchanan said. "And nobody's fool."

"Prettier than my daughter, Maria?"

"Prettier?" Buchanan asked thoughtfully. "I don't guess I'd try to compare the two of them."

"Why not? A woman is a woman."

Buchanan smiled down at the little woman. "Which you know isn't true, ma'am. Your daughter's more on the beauty side."

"You find that a detriment?"

"I don't rightly know what we're talking about," he said.

"Which *you* know isn't true."

"Which I can't even consider," Buchanan said.

"Then I will make you consider it. Will you marry my daughter?"

"No, ma'am."

"She is not worthy of you?"

"Let's not joke about this thing," Buchanan said gently.

"I'm sorry. If I told you I wanted you for Maria's husband, would that make a difference?"

"I could never make your daughter happy. Does that make a difference to you?"

"Maria's happiness is the goal of my life. It is all I live for."

"Then stop worrying about me."

"Believe me, Tomaso, I was not worried about you. I could not have been more pleased with a son-in-law than yourself. But if it cannot be, may I ask a mother's favor?"

"Anything."

"Let Maria know. Let her know certainly, for all time. Do not ride away as a man of romance and mystery. When she marries Sebastian Diaz let her give herself completely, without doubts about what might have been."

"I'll do the best I can," Buchanan promised.

CHAPTER SEVENTEEN

THE approach of a horse awoke the light-sleeping Abe Carbo and brought him to his feet all in one continuing motion. He peered out the small window of the hut but there was nothing at all to be seen in that utter blackness. The sound, however, kept growing, and what disturbed Carbo about it was the direction. The rider was arriving from the north.

Carbo buckled the gun at his waist, retrieved his hat and moved outside to his own picketed mount. Within seconds he was in pursuit of the man ahead, gauging the distance between them at three hundred feet and content to leave it at that until he knew their destination. For even though they were on Del Cuervo range it was still possible that the one ahead was just a wayfarer passing through the country innocently. Carbo doubted that that was the case, but he was willing to grant the man the outside chance. . . .

Amos Agry was oblivious to being followed. More than that, he was not even aware that he had passed quite close to a line camp and that there were still wisps of chimney smoke to reveal its occupancy. Like most men whose lives have been spent in or near towns, Amos was as much a stranger on the open range as he would have been in the center of the ocean. It was enough to point the horse in the desired direction and then to sit there until journey's end. He had even come on this particular journey unarmed.

Some thirty minutes later Amos did spy the unusual amount of light glowing from the Del Cuervo hacienda and the surrounding area. It told him that a fiesta was in full swing, and he considered that in appreciation of his timely warning to Buchanan, Don Pedro might very well invite him to join the festivities. Amos had heard much about the wild good time at these galas and the prospect of actually attending one caused him to quicken the mount's pace.

For Abe Carbo, the light up ahead served to silhouette the figure of the man he followed. There was a general conformity about it that was very familiar, and at the same time naggingly elusive. Then, in the same moment that Amos Agry spurred his horse, Carbo recognized him.

A sellout, he thought immediately. Simon had sent his cousin to dicker with Buchanan, perhaps offer him safe conduct to the north and freedom from prosecution for return of part of the money. It surprised Carbo that he had misread Simon's thought processes; surprised him and angered him as he set out to overtake the inexpert rider.

Amos Agry did not so much hear pursuit as he sensed it. Even so, by the time he looked over his shoulder and saw Carbo it was too late. Carbo's slim arm lashed out at him, in its hand a long slender blade that pierced his jugular vein, strangling the cry in his throat and pitching him headlong from the horse. Carbo was on him like a cat, turning him on his back and plunging the knife up under his ribs and into his heart. He wiped the blade clean on the rough fabric of Agry's woolen shirt, reflecting that under the circumstances it had been about the most efficient and noiseless murder he had ever done.

He sent Amos's horse running in the opposite direction, remounted his own and made his way cautiously toward the sounds of music and laughter at the hacienda.

If there was ever a beau-of-the-ball it would have to be Buchanan the night he danced at Don Pedro's *gran fiesta*. He was everywhere at once, and wherever he was, that's where the party was. He tilted jugs in contests with the vaqueros, he shook the maracas and led the orchestra, he kissed every woman in attendance and danced the fandango as it was never danced before.

"Incréible!" "Formidable!" "Impossible!" That's what they said of Buchanan as he let off a whole two years' supply of steam.

The night had actually begun rather solemnly, though a witness coming on the scene after midnight would have been hard pressed to believe it had been anything but bedlam from the start. The solemn occasion had taken place in the great hall of the hacienda. There, amid a handful of specially invited guests, Don Pedro had addressed himself to Buchanan.

"Amigo mio," he had said, "this night is yours. And so that you may always remember this fiesta held in your honor, those of us in your everlasting debt would like to present you with small mementos. First, my daughter Maria."

Maria had stepped forward and stood before Buchanan, her face and figure brilliant in the soft glow of the candle-lit room.

"Señor," the girl said huskily, "to you I owe my life and my future happiness." Then, from a small case she carried in her hands, she had taken a slender gold chain from which was suspended a wafer-thin golden heart. In the center of the heart was a diamond that must have weighed five carats. Buchanan bent down and Maria fastened the keepsake around his neck. She touched her lips fleetingly to his cheek.

"My son Juan," Pedro said, and the slender youth, garbed all in white, shook Buchanan's hand and spoke with great emotion. "Of everything that you did for me," he said, "I will always be most grateful for the gift of your understanding and moral courage during that long night we spent together in the cell. May this, amigo, remind you of my gratitude throughout your life." Juan's gift was a narrow belt of silver, the traditional identification of a Spanish hidalgo, and hanging from it was a sheathed, bejeweled dagger. He buckled the belt around Buchanan's waist, shook his hand again and stepped back.

"My friend and segundo, Gomez," Don Pedro said.

"I have a horse for you, Buchanan," Gomez announced, his gruff voice echoing through the room. "A white stallion with a spirit to match your own." The words lay there, unembellished, and Buchanan knew that he owned an animal very dear to Gomez's heart.

"Doña Isabel," Don Pedro said.

The little lady, wearing a diamond tiara which picked up the dancing lights, moved from her husband's side and looked up into the big man's face. "Wherever you travel, Tomaso *mío*, a mother's prayers will be with you. I can give you nothing more. But for the bride you will some day choose to share life with you, this token of my love for her."

The token was a gleaming sapphire necklace, twelve blue-green, perfectly matched stones, each the size of an almond. She showed it to Buchanan in its case, closed the lid and put it in his hand. Buchanan leaned over and received her kiss.

Don Pedro came and stood opposite him, tall and straight.

"My house," he said, "is your house. Your friends are my friends, your enemies are my enemies." He lifted Buchanan's left hand and on the third finger slipped an enormous gold ring marked with the signet of the Del Cuervo family. It made him, in effect, a member of the ancient clan and an heir to its fortunes.

A servant came forward bearing a goblet of wine. Don Pedro sipped from it and handed it to Buchanan. Buchanan drank thirstily, trying to clear the dryness in his throat.

"I hope you know," he said, "that I never felt so terrible in my life. There's a limit to what a man can take." The tremendous figure of the man, looming all black and solid, seemed to belie that statement. But there was a humbleness in his rich voice that made his listeners understand.

Buchanan had spoken directly to Don Pedro. Now, with a shift of his body, he addressed himself to the mother and son and daughter.

"A man like me has his limits," he said, paraphrasing what he had just said, giving it special meaning. "Yesterday a judge and a prosecutor took me along my back-trail and I came out of it looking like a pretty sorry specimen. Tonight you folks reverse the verdict." He lifted the goblet and drank again.

"Somebody," Buchanan said, looking directly at Maria, "would seem to be wrong. But the truth is, as I know Tom Buchanan, he's not quite so worthless as Lew Agry painted him for a jury, and not nearly the man the Del Cuervo family would like to imagine. Buchanan," Buchanan said, "is a bum. He's a restless, rootless drifter who knows a little bit about everybody else's business but not one damn thing about his own."

The servant came and filled the goblet to the brim. Buchanan all but drained it.

"You folks," he went on into that expectant silence, "have made quite a fuss tonight. You've thrown a fiesta just for me and you've given me gifts that I know are as precious as anything you own. Even so, I get the feeling that you're not satisfied. The trouble is, you let your emotions run away with your head. But it's going to be all right. I'll be gone tomorrow, on that white horse of Gomez's, loaded down with my loot, and day after tomorrow you'll settle down to the regular run of this establishment and be able to see things in their true light. You'll understand that Buchanan was just passing through, that he's of no more consequence than one of those shooting stars that goes whipping across the sky with a lot of fireworks tied to his tail. But the stars that you can count on are always there, and when the night's over the sun comes up just as regular as ever."

Buchanan turned his attention to Doña Isabel. "Ma'am, you gave me a necklace for my bride. You said it was for some girl who was going to share my life with me. I wish you'd take back the condition, because the life I see ahead has no place in it for a wife."

The lady nodded, telling him with her eyes that he had said all he need say so far as her daughter was concerned.

"And if it's agreeable," Buchanan said, "I hear the music starting up outside and this man's rarin' to go." He gave his arm to Doña Isabel and escorted her to the patio where he danced the first dance with her and then claimed Maria.

He found the girl in his arms mercurial, gay and vivacious, and as they whirled around the marble patio Buchanan had a moment's doubt about everything he'd said of himself in the hacienda. That moment ended when the music stopped and he released the girl to the stag line.

"Thank you, Buchanan, for everything," Maria said.

He and Gomez adjourned to the segundo's quarters then for a half hour's drinking with Ramon and the other top hands. Buchanan returned to find the first fandango being danced and the tall, smouldering-eyed girl from San Javier the center of attraction. He moved out toward her, grinning, and that was when the party began. Soon they were the only ones dancing, the others gathered round in a circle, keeping the beat with their hands, and when they finished a great *"Hola!"* went up. Then another as Buchanan bent the girl's lithe body to his and kissed her full on the lips.

"Where are you going, hombre?" Lilita called after the abruptly retreating figure, racing to catch up with him.

"Honey," he told her happily, "I'd forgotten what a woman felt like. Now I've got to quench the fire."

"I'll go with you."

"That won't quench it."

"Bueno!" she said, slipping her slim hand into his and leading him to one of the wine casks. There she filled two cups. First she drank from his, then held her own to his lips. Buchanan drank.

"There," she said. "It is done."

"What's done?"

"We are betrothed, you and I."

"The hell you say!"

"It is the custom."

"Hey, Gomez!" Buchanan yelled, but before the man could reach him the girl had slipped away into the shadows.

"What is it, amigo? You roar like a gored bull!"

"How do you get engaged in this country?"

"We have many ways," Gomez said with a twinkle. "The most interesting, they say, is to be surprised by the lady's father."

"How about if you drink her wine?"

Gomez shrugged. "That would interest me," he said, "but not very much. And speaking of wine . . ."

During the next hour Buchanan kept getting fleeting glimpses of the girl, each time surrounded by vaqueros, and when it came around to the traditional solo dances he watched from the shadows as she entertained with a tambourine and made her full skirts whirl and twist to her thighs. The crowd made her dance again, and the music grew wilder, and quite unexpectedly Buchanan looked up to find her before him, her breasts heaving beneath the thin blouse she wore, her hands offering a drink from her cup of wine.

Buchanan emptied it, threw the cup away and reached for the girl. They kissed, but when he would have kissed her again she slipped away from him and ran for the bordering grove. And he might never have found her if she hadn't betrayed her dark hiding place by a soft musical laugh.

They were together then for what seemed to them both was an instant and an eternity and afterward Buchanan was content to lie on that soft earth forever, his face buried against her sweet-smelling breasts. . . .

"I'm going to get dressed," Lilita announced suddenly.

"Why?"

"Because I want to dance one more time. In front of everyone, but just for you alone."

"You can dance for me alone right here."

"This is different. It is important to me."

So she dressed and they rejoined the fiesta. Lilita spoke to the musicians and they struck up a tempo that was unfamiliar to Buchanan's ears. The girl danced to it, slowly, sensuously, and though Buchanan watched her pleasurably he was conscious that the other onlookers were glancing at him just as often as they did her.

"So, amigo?" Gomez said at his elbow. "You have found an interesting way of your own?"

"Is that what she's telling all these folks?" Buchanan asked in amazement.

"Not quite. That is an ancient dance she is doing. I am surprised that she even knew it. What she is saying is farewell to the other vaqueros who courted her."

"Lucky for me I'm pulling stakes," Buchanan said.

Gomez slapped him on the back. "You don't

sound like you feel so lucky, hombre," he told him. "Come on, it is time for two bachelors to do some serious drinking." They picked up Ramon on the way, and Buchanan returned from that visit to headquarters without a care in the world. It was then that he personally undertook the success of the fiesta.

CHAPTER EIGHTEEN

NEXT to Lilita, no one was enjoying the performance of El Hombre more than Maria del Cuervo. Buchanan danced with her audaciously, holding her close, flinging her about, manhandling her as no vaquero would have dared. He had even persuaded her to dance alone, to Don Pedro's amazement, then happily scandalized all Rancho del Rey by rewarding her with a firm kiss.

"Be at ease," Doña Isabel told her husband. "Our daughter is coming of age on a wonderful night. This is her last fling before marriage to Sebastian Diaz."

"So, *bella mia*. And did you have your fling before our wedding night?"

His wife matched his smile. "You are not Sebastian," she said, and thought: Nor was there Buchanan.

"*Ai!*" Don Pedro said. "Your child is going to shake her hips again."

"Good. Perhaps she wants to be kissed again. Where are you going, husband?"

Don Pedro had arisen. "Buchanan," he said, "has desecrated our native dances enough. I am going to demonstrate the fandango as it is done in Madrid." So saying he joined his daughter on the floor, to the cheers of his people, and when the dance was done it was he who was kissed.

But that ended Maria's activity for the night. The doctor had decreed a midnight curfew, and now it was an hour past that time. The girl returned to the hacienda willingly, conscious of weariness, and Felice attended her until she was in bed.

"Now whom do you go to meet?" Maria asked, and the Indian giggled.

"Oh, that Ramon!" she said. "He has been flirting with me the whole night . . ."

"You could not do better," Maria said. "He is Café's favorite and certain to succeed him."

"I do love him, I think," Felice said. "Only tonight I worry if it is me or the wine. Good night, señorita."

"Good hunting, Felicita," Maria said drowsily and the servant left to join Ramon, who waited in the kitchen.

Carbo left the horse at a safe distance and observed the fiesta from the edge of the grove. He noted the movements of Buchanan and Gomez, of Don Pedro and Juan, then skirted the lighted area and worked his way around behind the big house. He entered by a rear door, mounted the narrow servants' stairway and let himself out on the corridor of the second floor.

Then, room by room, he made his search for the one Buchanan occupied and the money he thought would be hidden there. The fourth door he opened was Maria's.

"Did you forget something, Felice?"

"An error," Carbo said in Spanish. "Go to sleep."

"Whose voice is that? I do not recognize it!"

"Be quiet!" Carbo hissed. "I leave in peace."

But Maria was too full of her ordeal with Roy Agry. She screamed. Carbo stepped quickly to the bed, sought her throat with his hands. At his touch Maria screamed again, threw herself away from him. Then Carbo was atop her, cutting off further sound, but from beyond the room he could hear someone's frenzied approach

Ramon never had a chance for his life. He came into the room and halted, his body framed in the doorway by the corridor light. Carbo fired at point-blank range, drove three slugs into that defenseless target, watched it sink to the floor and then stepped over it to make his escape down the corridor. Felice had reached the top of the staircase. She and Carbo stared at each other for one terrible moment. Then the gun swung up and roared its message.

Carbo watched the girl plunge back down the stairs with an expression of vast disbelief. He had killed without reason, without reason at all. The same in the room. This was panic. He had to get himself under control, had to get out of here. . . .

It had been one of the rare occasions when the musicians were not playing. Maria's screams came down to those on the patio with terrifying clarity, sounds so incompatible with the general gaiety that for a brief time nearly every mind

167

was paralyzed. The nearest entrance to the hacienda was at the rear, and Buchanan and Gomez broke for it even as the gunshots sounded inside. In pure reflex, both men slapped for guns they were not carrying this night, cursed the circumstances and kept right on coming. Buchanan opened the door and mounted the stairs three at a time. In the corridor two more shots racketed. Footsteps pounded their way, and Buchanan stepped directly into Carbo's path.

The gun went off in his face, so close that his skin felt the heat of the muzzle blast. But the slug itself screamed past his ear, crashed into the wall behind him, and then there were the dull clicks of an empty gun being triggered. Both Buchanan and Carbo looked at the Colt, unable to comprehend what had happened. Then Carbo threw the heavy revolver at the other man and snatched the wicked-looking knife from his belt.

"Back off! I'm coming through!"

Buchanan unsheathed the dress dagger Juan had given him. As he did Garbo thrust his leg forward, caught it behind Buchanan's calf and jerked him off balance. The blade in Carbo's hand arched upward, passed harmlessly through the air. Two years with Campos's ruffians had schooled Buchanan for this combat, taught him how to fall away and turn the other man's attack against him. Before Carbo could strike again Buchanan drove the dagger hilt-deep into his belly. Carbo sighed, fell against Buchanan's shoulder and then dropped to the floor. Gomez streaked past them toward Maria's room.

Gomez's anguished cry echoed and re-echoed in Buchanan's ears. He went to the room himself, found Maria unharmed but the segundo bent down over the bullet-gutted body of Ramon. Soon the room was filling with people. Don Pedro made his way to Buchanan's side.

"What is it? What has occurred?"

"I don't know," Buchanan said. "I can't understand it."

Gomez turned his face up to them. "I charge Ramon's death," he said unsteadily, "to Simon Agry."

"But why?" Don Pedro asked. "What is the purpose of this tragedy?"

Gomez got to his feet, moved between them and on out of the room.

"Gomez!" Don Pedro called. "Where are you going?"

"To repay this visit, señor. Please do not try to stop me."

"But you have been drinking the whole night. You cannot organize yourself. You cannot ride."

"I am sober, Don Pedro." He looked at Buchanan. "Amigo, this is not your affair. Do you understand?"

"Yes. But you ought to wait."

Gomez shook his head stubbornly, turned to the assembled vaqueros. "Who rides with me?" he asked, and when he walked away they followed him to a man.

Simon Agry had found it a night when sleep wouldn't come. There were so many things that had gone wrong for him, so much to worry about and keep his mind fretfully awake. And all in one day.

Where, tonight, was the dream he had nourished of being lord and master of the vast Rancho del Rey? Where was the gold that was going to buy the great herds of cattle and horses, the same stock that he would sell to the government at such a big profit when he was in Washington to negotiate the contracts? Where was Abe Carbo? What success would he have raising gunmen? And always the big vexation: Would Buchanan actually stay in the country with all that money in his possession?

He also cursed his kin. Brother Lew for his perfidy, his stupid acts of treachery that had brought Simon to this terrible brink of disaster, and Cousin Amos for leaving town when Simon needed an outlet for his wrath.

Simon tossed and turned heavily in his bed and couldn't induce sleep. So he finally got up and went out onto the porch, to smoke a cigar and let his self-pity and anger have its full play. Thus it was, in the almost total silence, that he heard the furious, frightening thunder of many horses to the south.

The south! Simon didn't stop to reason why Don Pedro was sending a force against him. He returned to his room and dressed in feverish haste.

Nor did he bawl orders to have his buggy rigged. Some sixth sense told him that it was safer to go off into the brush on foot, safer to keep his whereabouts a secret even from his own men.

And where were they? Not one of them stirred from the blacked-out bunkhouse, though the sound of the oncoming riders seemed almost deafening to Simon Agry. Oh, God, where was Abe Carbo? Where was Lew? He was suddenly flooded with affection for his dead brother.

Simon went away from the house and hurried toward the thick forest of scrub pine that grew some three hundred feet away.

Esteban Gomez was a grim and vengeful man as he rode at the head of his band into Agrytown. Like Don Pedro and Buchanan he did not understand why they had been attacked by a lone assassin. All he did know was that Ramon and a girl servant had been wantonly killed, that Abe Carbo was Simon Agry's man, and that his anger was full of tears.

He swept into Agry's yard, dismounted and entered the house alone while his men surrounded the bunkhouse, firing into it and hazing the sleepy-eyed occupants outside.

A minute later Gomez reappeared on the porch. Behind him, through the windows, flame was visible and at sight of it two vaqueros disappeared into the bunkhouse. When they returned, that too was afire and they rode out. The search for Simon Agry continued in the town proper — in the hotel, the saloon, the mercantile, the bank — and each place that they failed to find him they put to the torch.

There was no shouting, no sound of victory, only the roar of the flames as the dry wooden buildings caught like so much fresh tinder. The hotel, the dominant structure, seemed to burn with a special vengeance, although Gomez and his men would never know just how disastrous a blow they were dealing Simon Agry with the destruction of that building.

It was dawn when Buchanan came through, and though a pall of smoke still lingered in the air there was nothing of any substance left in Agrytown to burn. He remembered his first impression of the place, of the impermanence of it, but not even in his most vivid imaginings would he have guessed that Agrytown would disappear in a night.

Buchanan slowed the big white stallion to a walk, for up ahead, squarely across his route, stood the lone figure of Simon Agry. Agry was hatless, and his hair was wild and disheveled. He wore a faded old shirt, and farmer's overalls, and Buchanan stared, thinking of the proud and arrogant figure in the campaign poster, the formidable judge looking down at everyone from his lofty bench.

"Hard times, mister," Buchanan said, stopping. And though Agry's lips moved no sound came immediately.

"My — my money," he finally managed to say. "A part of it. Give me just enough for a stake."

"I have nothing of yours," Buchanan told him.

"My money," Agry repeated tonelessly, his eyes dull in his face. "You took it — took it from my brother."

Buchanan shook his head, jerked his thumb over his shoulder at the ashen ruin that had been the hotel.

"I got my purse back," he said. "The rest was in the saddlebags. I couldn't have dragged them with me if I'd wanted to."

Agry was hearing the truth and enough of it was getting through to his shocked mind. "My cousin," he said haltingly. "Amos took it . . ."

"Amos is dead," Buchanan said. "So is Carbo. Neither of them had your money." He turned his head around and glanced curiously at the hotel site, suspecting what had happened. Then he reached into his purse, grabbed a handful of coins at random and handed them down.

"All I can spare, mister," he said. "I sweated blood for every dollar of it."

Agry grasped at the gold without a word of thanks. Buchanan shrugged and rode on, washing his hands of the whole trouble. Along the trail, however, there was a steady succession of reminders. Emerson's shack, the places where they had paused on the way to the river, the river itself. It was midday when he reached there and stopped to water the horse and eat his meal. He pushed on then along the road that skirted the river and crossed it via a bridge, riding marveling at the simple fact that he was actually putting distance between himself and Mexico.

Free, that's what he was, but somehow his freedom wasn't everything he had hoped it would be. There was something missing. Buchanan rode on, and the sun that had started with him over his right shoulder now cast long shadows from the left. He pulled off the trail and found a suitable camp for the night. Soon his cook-fire was the only light there was, and after his supper he sat with his smoke and gazed thoughtfully into the embers.

"What do you see?" asked a soft voice and Buchanan thought he had been mesmerized by the fire. But the hand that lay on his shoulder was real enough.

Buchanan's fingers closed over the slim wrist and pulled the copper-haired girl down across his knees.

"Lilita, you're as loco as I am."

"I know, Buchanan."

"Had anything to eat?" he asked and she smiled up at him lazily.

"Hombre," she said. "I did not come all this way to eat."

William R. Cox was born in Peapack, New Jersey. His early career was in newspaper journalism. In the late 1930s he began writing sports, crime, and adventure stories for the magazine market, and he made his debut as a Western writer with "Night of the Blood Bucket Raid" in *Dime Western* in the January, 1941 issue. It is worth noting that his Western story debut was with the first of several stories to feature a series character, Terry Glenn. During the 1940s Cox created a number of other series characters for the magazine market, most notably the Whistler Kid who appeared regularly in *10 Story Western* and Duke Bagley whose adventures usually were featured in *Star Western*. "The short story form was blissful until there were no markets," he once recalled. In the 1950s and 1960s Cox turned to television and wrote at least a hundred teleplays for such series as "Broken Arrow," "Dick Powell's Zane Grey Theatre," "The Virginian," and "Bonanza." He also won a host of readers writing original paperback Western novels, the best known of which are novels about the adventures of two series characters originally published by Fawcett Gold Medal: Cemetery Jones in a series published under his own byline and the Tom Buchanan series which appeared under the house name, Jonas Ward. Dale L. Walker in the second edition of TWENTIETH CENTURY WESTERN WRITERS commented that William R. Cox's Western "novels are noted for their 'pageturner' pace, realistic dialogue, and frequent Colt-and-Winchester gun play. The series of novels built around the strong West Texas character, Tom Buchanan, are very typical Cox Westerns."